THE NANNY'S CHILD

BOOKS BY L.G. DAVIS

THE LIES WE TELL SERIES

The New Nanny

Liar Liar

Perfect Parents

My Husband's Secret

The Missing Widow

The Stolen Breath

Don't Blink

The Midnight Wife

The Janitor's Wife

THE NANNY'S CHILD

L.G. DAVIS

bookouture

Published by Bookouture in 2023

An imprint of Storyfire Ltd.
Carmelite House
50 Victoria Embankment
London EC4Y 0DZ

www.bookouture.com

ISBN: 978-1-83790-472-3
eBook ISBN: 978-1-83790-471-6

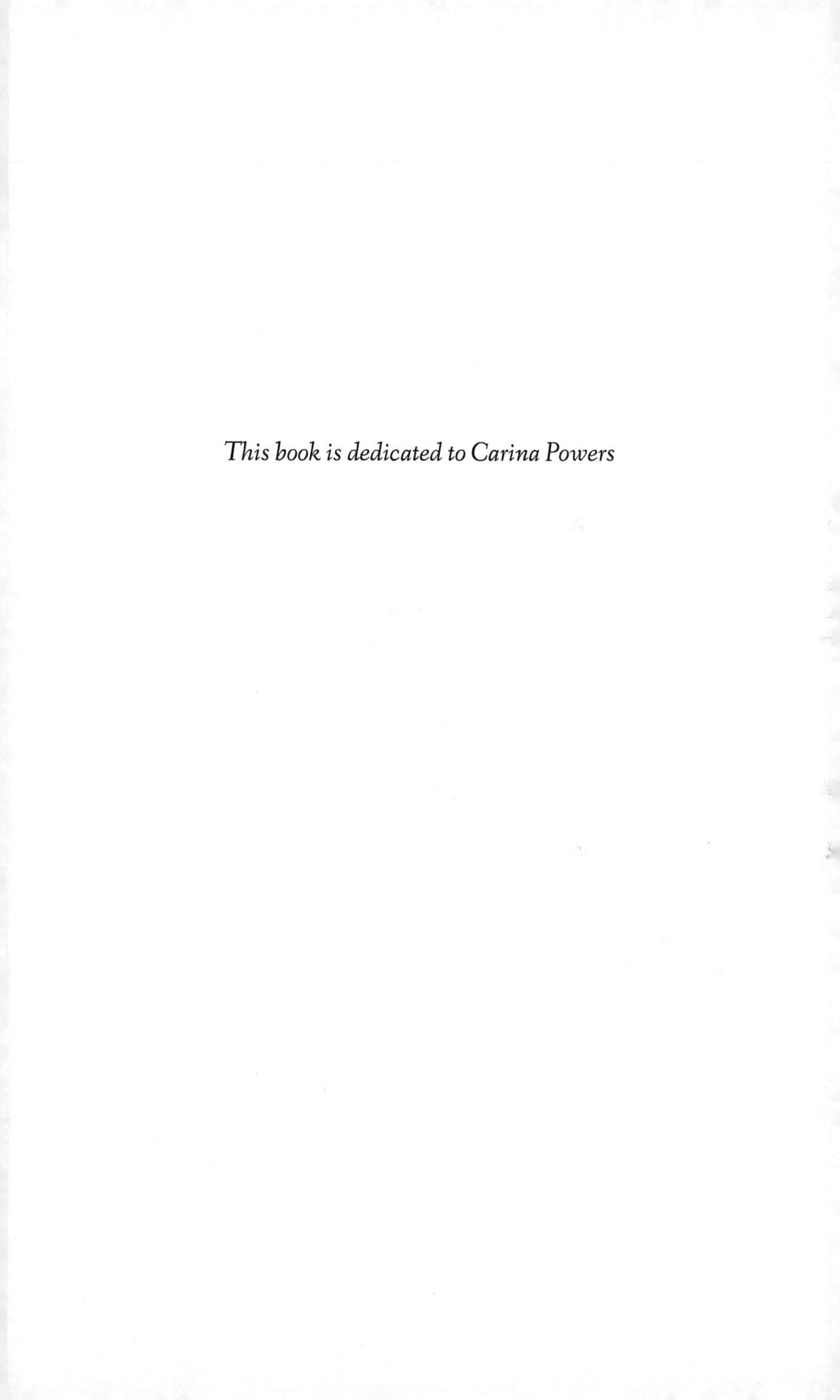

This book is dedicated to Carina Powers

PROLOGUE

As soon as the gun is aimed at the spot between my eyebrows, I know today is the last day of my life.

It's possible that the person holding the gun will change their mind and spare me, but I doubt it. Perhaps it's the look in their eyes, or the way they're gripping the handle so tightly; I know in my heart that my time has run out.

A million regrets and memories flash through my mind: all the things I should have done differently; all the ways I should have loved more; all the moments I should have treasured.

As I gaze into the barrel, I suddenly feel as if I'm looking into a portal, a doorway to the afterlife. My forehead is slick with sweat, and I'm trying to slow my breathing, but every second feels like an eternity. My mind is filled with questions I would never have dreamed of asking. How will it feel to be shot? Will it be quick? How painful will it be? Will I feel the bullet rip through my skull, or will everything instantly fade to black?

As fear takes over, I no longer hear the noise of the world. All that's left is the sound of my rapidly beating heart.

Every detail of my murderer catches my attention—the

color of their eyes, the shape of their lips, the slight wrinkle on their forehead. It's strange, noticing all these details when I'm about to die. My mind seems to be clutching onto every last bit of life that it can.

The other person must be experiencing a million emotions and thoughts. Maybe they have regrets and wishes, like I do. Do they regret what they're about to do?

The clock continues to tick toward the end of my time among the living, and I wait for the inevitable. But even in the face of death, I can't help but feel a sudden urge to fight, to not give up so easily. Especially when I think of my girls and never being able to see them again. I'm not ready to die, not yet.

My body tenses up and a sudden burst of energy courses through me. I take a step forward, surprising the other person. Their eyes widen with shock and confusion. I don't know where the courage comes from, but I grab onto it and ride it.

As my killer tries to gather themselves, I grab onto the hand holding the gun. The force of my movement catches them off guard, but they don't let go of the weapon.

Instead, they tighten their grip, trying to maintain control. For a moment, we're locked in a deadly dance, each struggling for control over the firearm until our bodies collide with the floor.

My adrenaline is surging, clouding my vision and heightening my senses. I'm not thinking, only acting on instinct. It's as if all my primal instincts have kicked in, and I fight with every ounce of strength I have left. I can feel the gun pressed against my skin now, but I don't let go. I'm not sure how long we're wrestling on the floor—it could be seconds or minutes—but finally a gunshot pierces the air.

I now know how it feels to be shot. It's like being struck by pure fire. The pain is blinding, a searing, burning heat emanating from my abdomen and radiating throughout my entire body.

If someone were to ask me how it feels to die, I would describe death as a slow, gradual drift into nothingness. As the pain intensifies, my senses start to dull; sounds and colors blend together into a garbled mix, and my vision grows darker around the edges.

I hear a distant ringing in my ears and I can feel warm blood oozing from the wound.

As the darkness creeps in, I suddenly start floating downwards into the unknown. A wave of serenity passes over me and I close my eyes, no longer feeling anything at all. Before everything fades away, all I remember is the face of the person that shot me. They will live with the guilt of what they did for the rest of their life. Or perhaps they won't feel remorse at all.

No matter how it turns out, I will no longer be here to see it.

My fight is over. The living must go on without me. But I worry about the girls. Who will watch over them when I'm gone? Who will protect them?

ONE

CHRISTA

When a child's wailing pierces the air, I know it's one of the twins. Ella or Leah—it's hard to tell from where I'm sitting. I'm still learning to tell them apart, and it doesn't make it easy that they're wearing identical outfits from head to toe, like two peas in a pod. Even their hair is the same shade of dark brown and falls into neat little bobs. It always takes me a moment to pick up on the subtle differences in the seven-year-old girls' facial features.

My eyes sweep the indoor playground before landing on the bright-red jungle gym by the swings.

I've been to many playgrounds in my life, but nothing as luxurious as Cedar Lane Playground in the center of Esterford, Kentucky. It's a child's dream come true, with a sandbox, a climbing wall, monkey bars, and even a mini zoo. Water features like fountains, brooks, and a pond bring the playground to life, making it feel like an enchanted wonderland.

Though it's November and cold outside, the space has been designed in a way that brings the outdoors inside. The jungle gym towers over the other structures, a bright beacon that calls out to adventurous children.

I rise from the white bench, careful not to wake Heather, who just closed her eyes a minute ago to take a nap. How my six-month-old can sleep through all the noise and commotion of the playground is beyond me, but I'm grateful for the reprieve.

I make my way over to the jungle gym, dodging children and parents chatting on picnic blankets spread out on the synthetic grass that looks so real it's almost impossible to tell it's not. The smell of popcorn and cotton candy from a nearby concession stand fills my nose, making my mouth water. I make a mental note to buy some treats for the girls to enjoy on the drive home.

The screams grow as I approach the jungle gym. It's definitely one of the twins. Leah, the younger twin, is stuck at the top of the slide. To tell them apart, I gave her a pink bow and Ella a yellow one. The little girl's face is red and blotchy from crying.

With Heather tied around my body in a wrap, I can't reach out to her, but I can't let her stay up there either.

"Hey there, Leah, what's wrong?" In an effort to ease her distress, I keep my voice calm and soothing.

She looks at me with wet eyes, her bottom lip quivering. "I can't slide down. I'm too scared." Her hair is matted with sweat, and her dress sticks to her body.

"All right, sweetheart. I know it can be scary up there. Do you want to come down?" I wonder if I can get someone to help. Most of the parents are busy with their own children or lost in conversations.

Leah nods, still sniffling. "I'm afraid of heights."

"It's fine, honey. Don't panic. I'll help you down."

"I can help her," Ella chimes in, appearing at my side, her hands on her hips.

"Are you sure?" I place a hand on the top of her head. I want to make sure that both girls are safe.

She nods confidently. "I've done it before."

"Okay, I'll stay here in case you need any help." I give her a thumbs up, impressed by her bravery.

Slowly and carefully, she climbs up the steps, her little hands gripping onto the shiny bars. She reaches the top and talks to her sister, encouraging her to let go and slide down with her as I move to stand at the base of the slide, ready to catch the girls if needed.

Leah looks hesitant, but with a gentle push from her sister, she eventually lets go and screams as she slides down. Ella follows closely behind, letting out a giggle when she joins her twin at the bottom.

When Leah starts clapping for herself, I pull her to my side. "Well done, you did it! You were so brave up there."

She looks up at me with a big smile, her fear replaced by excitement. "Thank you, Christa. I'm not scared anymore."

I smile back at her. "Glad to hear it, kiddo."

The sight of children enjoying themselves always fills me with joy; however, I know I mustn't get too attached.

As much as I find the twins adorable, I can't afford to lock them inside my heart, like I did at my last job—an experience that ended terribly. But the main reason why I can't do this is because I'm not planning to stay.

In a few weeks, I'll be out of their lives forever. I'm still not sure how I came to be here in the first place. Every time I think about it, something creeps up my spine, sending chills to my fingertips.

As the girls go off to play again, I walk back to the bench, wrapping my arms around my baby as I glance behind me, like I do every single day, peering over my shoulder to see if I'm being watched. It always feels that way.

In the sea of faces, I don't see anyone, or anything suspicious, but I know he's out there. I may not see or hear him, but I can feel the sensation of his gaze on my skin and the hairs rise at the nape of my neck and my arms.

I don't know if it was him who sent me that note, three weeks ago, which led to me being here, working as a nanny again after I'd decided to quit the profession. The note had been left in my mailbox and it had a name and an address typed on it, along with a message that said: "What you're looking for is here."

At first, I thought it was some kind of sick joke, but something inside me compelled me to follow through with it. As soon as I saw the owner of the house, I knew I needed to stay, to find out more. Until I get answers. Some may call me crazy, but I wouldn't be doing this if my life didn't depend on it. I'm still shocked that I got the job despite me being a new mom.

While still keeping my attention on the girls, who are now at the swings, I feel Heather move against my chest, her warmth seeping into my skin. I close my eyes for a brief moment, savoring the feeling of her tiny body in my arms.

The first few days after she was born, I lived with the fear that something would go wrong, that my baby would be taken from me again. But she's still with me, and I'm grateful for every moment that I have with her.

Half an hour later, I press my lips to the top of her head and stand up again, calling the girls to let them know it's time to go home.

During the twenty-minute drive, while the twins are enjoying their cotton candy, I admire the town.

Esterford oozes with charm and serenity, giving off a sense of peace and tranquility. It's a stark contrast to New York, where I found the streets crowded, noisy, and filled with fake smiles. I take in the scenery, the trees swaying gently in the breeze, the quaint little shops lining the streets. Colors shift from bright and bold to muted pastels.

Driving through the square, I spot the famous Esterford Fortress, tall and proud, standing against the backdrop of the setting sun. Inside it is the local bank, the mayor's office, and a small museum.

The structure, with its towering walls and turrets, has stood there for centuries, bearing witness to countless stories, secrets, and mysteries. I heard that the town's celebrations and festivals are often held there, and it's a popular spot for tourists to take pictures. Despite the beauty of the attraction, to me it's a reminder of Austria, the land of castles and palaces, where I spent the most terrifying summer of my life.

As my stomach clenches, I push aside the dark memories and focus on the present. To distract myself, I turn on the radio, choosing a children's station that's already playing Christmas songs.

The twins sing along to "Jingle Bells" and "Rudolph the Red-Nosed Reindeer", while Heather giggles, her hands flailing in the air. I smile, captivated by the way her face lights up, forgetting for a moment the troubles that linger in my mind.

We turn the corner to our street, and less than a minute later we pull into the driveway of Harper and Troy Wells' house. It's a beautiful, two-story Victorian on the lake with its own dock and a pristine, white boat that proudly bobs in the water.

I couldn't believe it when they showed me the guest cottage on their land where they wanted me to stay. I've been a live-in nanny before, but never had my own private cottage, a cozy retreat that feels like it's been plucked from a storybook. It has windows with red shutters, a small porch with a rocking chair, and a roof with a chimney at one end.

Inside, the walls are painted a soft cream color, and the furniture is a mix of antique and modern pieces that somehow work perfectly together. Two arched windows look out onto the lake. Since it was in the evening when I arrived, I could see the sun setting over the water in the distance, and couldn't wait to wake up to that view in the morning.

The girls are quick to unbuckle their seatbelts and jump out of the car, eager to show off their cotton-candy-stained faces to their parents. I grab Heather's car seat and follow them to the ornate, wooden front door, my heart pounding with anticipation.

As soon as the door opens and Troy is standing there, my stomach clenches.

He's a very handsome man, with sharp cheekbones, a chiseled jawline, and piercing blue eyes. His sandy-blond hair is styled perfectly and, despite the casual attire of a t-shirt and jeans, he looks like he just walked off a movie set. Over his t-shirt, he's wearing an apron, which says "World's Best Husband" in bold letters, a sure sign that he's been cooking something in the kitchen.

I'm actually surprised to see him home before eight. As the only pediatrician in town with his own practice, he's usually busy until late in the evening.

"Hello girls, you're just in time for dinner." Troy laughs as he lifts his daughters into his arms and gives them each a kiss on the cheek.

"Hi, Christa." He looks at me with a smile and his eyes linger on my face for a moment too long. I smile back.

"Hi, Troy." I can feel the heat rising to my cheeks as I try to avoid his gaze.

He's been looking at me like this from the moment I arrived —gazing for just a second too long as if he's wondering something about me, but he never says a word.

As soon as we enter the house, the air smells of roasted chicken and curry spice, making my stomach growl in hunger. I follow Troy and the girls through the dining room and into the kitchen, where Harper is sitting at the island, her mouse-brown hair pulled up into a messy bun as she leafs through a fashion magazine.

A delicate gold necklace hangs from her neck. The pendant

hanging from it is a simple teardrop shape, with an intricate design of swirls and diamonds embedded in the surface.

She's a stunning woman with shoulder-length brown hair, almond-shaped eyes the color of hazelnut, and full, pouty lips that always seem to be painted in a shade of red. At twenty-seven, she's fifteen years younger than Troy, but despite the freckles on her nose that make her look like a little girl, the way she carries herself makes her appear much older.

She hugs the twins, then looks at me with a dimpled smile. "I hope the girls didn't give you a hard time, Christa."

"No, of course not. They were amazing." I leave out the part where Leah was stuck on the jungle gym, because I learned quickly that she's one of those mothers who freaks out about every little scratch.

Troy laughs out loud and turns to his wife. "Do you believe her, baby?"

Harper laughs along with him, her smile wide and bright. "Oh, I don't know, Troy. I think she's got what it takes to handle our little troublemakers." She winks at me.

Troy nods. "Well, then you'll fit right in with us, Christa. We're a family of troublemakers." When our eyes meet, his narrow just a little, and I can see a flicker of something in them again, but then, as soon as it appears, it's gone.

I wonder again if he recognizes me. When we were introduced by Harper, I expected him to say something—to tell me to leave—but he welcomed me into his home like I was a part of his family.

I watch as he goes to wrap an arm around Harper, pulling her close to his side. "Baby, can I get you anything to drink?" he asks, his voice low and husky as he brushes a kiss against her temple.

Harper shakes her head, her fingers tracing the design on her necklace. "Only if Christa can join me." She turns to me.

"Would you like to share a drink before dinner is ready? Troy is not the fastest cook, and food won't be ready for a while."

As we speak, the twins race past us, giggling as they disappear around the corner. I can't help but feel a pang of envy at the way Troy and Harper interact. They seem so comfortable with each other; so in love.

"Sure," I say, trying to shake off the feeling of jealousy. "But Heather still needs to be fed, so I'll just have some juice for now."

In the kitchen, Troy returns to the stove while Harper and I sit at the island, sipping our drinks while Heather is on a playmat on the floor close to me.

Harper leans in. "There's nothing sexier than a man who can cook. I don't know how I got so lucky."

I nod in agreement, taking another sip of my wine. "You are such a lovely couple with the perfect marriage."

"Perfect? Far from it," Harper laughs. "We've had our fair share of ups and downs, but we always manage to work through it together."

"I've been meaning to ask, how did you two meet?"

Harper's gaze takes on a faraway look, as if she's reminiscing. "I was studying social work at the University of Kentucky, and he was a resident doctor at a hospital nearby."

"Tell her what you were doing when we met," Troy interjects, a playful grin on his face as he joins us at the island. But he doesn't give her a chance to answer. "I was driving past the university when I saw her handing out homemade sandwiches to students who couldn't afford lunch. I was immediately drawn to her kindness and selflessness." He brushes a hand over Harper's shoulder, and she leans into him, smiling.

"I remember that day," Harper says, her voice soft. "You stopped and asked me if I needed help, and we ended up talking for hours. Now here we are."

"That's a really beautiful story. It's like fate brought you two together."

Troy chuckles. "Or maybe it was just hunger that brought me to her. Those sandwiches were pretty amazing."

Dinner is served half an hour later, and the entire time I watch Troy move around the kitchen with ease, his broad shoulders shifting as he plates the food. The scent of spices and herbs fills the air, making my mouth water. As I take a bite of the chicken, my taste buds explode with flavor.

As we eat, they continue telling me their love story, how they'd eloped and got married in a homeless shelter where Harper used to volunteer. She had wanted the homeless people to whom she'd grown close to be a part of their special day. Troy had happily obliged.

"My wife is a beautiful woman." Troy beams at Harper. "But it's her caring heart that makes her truly stunning. She made those people feel seen and loved. It was one of the most incredible things I've ever witnessed."

Harper reaches for her wine and takes a sip. "And you cried like a baby during our vows."

Troy laughs, but doesn't deny it. "I couldn't help it. The moment was just so damn perfect, and the shelter had bucketloads of food after the reception. It was a win-win situation."

"It was special." Harper refills Leah's glass with apple juice. "I loved that everyone dressed up for the occasion."

After dinner, on my way to the cottage, the hairs at the back of my neck rise, and I turn to scan the surroundings. A woman is standing by the window of the house across the street, holding what looks like a glass of wine and watching me intently. She's very tall and lean, with jet-black hair that falls in waves past her shoulders.

Harper told me that her name is Madison Baker, and I get the impression that they have a closer relationship than with the other neighbors, as Madison stops by almost every day, though never for long, and she usually only interacts with Harper in the driveway. I guess a quick chat is all they need to exchange news and check in with each other.

They also have the same style. More than once in the past week, I've seen Madison wear clothes that were exact replicas of Harper's.

I turn around quickly, pretending I haven't seen her. The last thing I want is to draw attention to myself while I'm here. Troy may not remember me... but I know him. And I'm here to find out the truth.

TWO

MADISON

I swallow a mouthful of Pinot Noir to chase away the taste of the pepperoni pizza I had for dinner, my gaze on the new nanny as she scurries to her cottage with the baby. Her steps are quick and there's an urgency in her movements, as if she's running from something.

Maybe she is.

I don't know what it is, but something about her sets my teeth on edge. From the moment she stepped into Harper's life a week ago, I didn't trust her. And it creeps me out that she tends to only wear black clothes each and every day.

No matter how hard I try, I can never understand how Harper would hire a nanny with an infant to take care of her kids. Even though she's always ready to help those in need, I frankly think hiring a nanny with a baby is going too far. She could easily have pointed her to one of her many charities.

There are too many red flags for me. First, the old nanny leaves abruptly, and then the new one shows up in an instant? It just doesn't add up. Harper is a generous soul, and I'm here to make sure nobody takes advantage of her kindness.

When the nanny disappears into the cottage, I stay in place, my eyes trained on the suddenly lit interior. I can't make out any details from this distance, so I reach for my binoculars and raise them to my face. The cottage comes into sharp focus, and I can now see everything happening inside with startling clarity.

As I watch her pace back and forth with her baby in her arms, I can tell that she is agitated about something. She lowers the child into a bassinet near the couch. Her lips are moving, like she's saying something to the baby or maybe singing.

I've yet to exchange words with her, but I have a bad feeling about why she's here, and I intend to get to the bottom of it.

I know everyone in this neighborhood and all their secrets.

As one of the few unmarried women on the street, I'm aware that many of the married ladies worry I might be out to steal their husbands. But marriage just isn't for me. Even when I was a little girl who was supposed to dream about wearing white and strolling down the aisle, I never wanted any part of it. A husband would only hold me back from living life on my own terms. Plus, I don't need a man to validate my worth as a woman. Alone, I've always been free to pursue whatever, and whomever, I want.

Rather than being tethered to a man who's passing the time until they find something better, I'm much more content being single—as nice as it would be to be invited to their lavish parties or their endless fundraisers.

Harper, however, is different from all the others.

The instant I saw her, when she and Troy were settling into their new home nine years ago, I knew we would be friends. I'm not sure what it was—how relaxed and content she seemed, the spark in her eyes when we first spoke, or her good heart—but eventually we formed a bond so strong that we might as well be sisters.

I'm not the most popular person in the neighborhood, and the other neighbors gossiped about me to her, trying to turn her against me. But Harper never listened to their lies and always stood by my side. She saw past their pettiness and judgment, something a true friend would do.

But it was when my German shepherd, Oscar, died that I really saw what a compassionate person she is. She created a beautiful memorial service in her own backyard, and although none of the neighbors showed up, it didn't matter. We sat together, drinking wine and sharing memories of my furry friend until the early hours of the morning.

At the time, I had only been living in the area for a year, and since my mom and friends from college don't live nearby, I was very much in need of a friend.

I take a break from watching the nanny to refill my glass of wine. When I return to the window, she's sitting on the couch with the baby on her lap, rocking her back and forth. Then she suddenly looks up and it's as if she's staring directly at me through the pane of glass. I quickly duck out of view and close the curtains.

I'll take a break for now, but I'm keeping an eye on her. If I see something suspicious, I'll tell Harper right away. Then she'll know that I have her back no matter what.

Sitting on my bed, I pull out my phone and scroll through my recent pictures until I see the nanny's face. I took the picture a few days ago, trying to capture as much detail as possible without compromising the resolution.

"Who are you and what are you doing here?" I whisper.

Reaching for my notepad and pencil, I review the notes I've been compiling. I have very little information. To learn more I'd have to get closer to her, to have a conversation with her. But whatever I do, I have to be careful.

We all have secrets, every single one of us. Some are bigger than others and some are harmless. It's possible that the woman means no harm, but once I find out who she is, I'll be the judge of that. I'll decide for myself whether she deserves to be around Harper and her children.

Still clutching my phone, I head to my sewing room across from my bedroom, the same room my paternal grandmother used for sewing her own handmade projects before she passed away and left me the house.

As a child, I used to love spending time here, watching Grandma June work on her creations and listening to her stories. Now, it's my haven—a place where I can reflect and organize my thoughts.

I settle at the desk that's covered in fabric scraps and unfinished projects.

Behind me, covering an entire wall, are shelves filled with spools of colorful thread, buttons, and ribbons. Since I didn't want it to look like any ordinary sewing room, I've also added a few shelves of antique figurines and knick-knacks that I've collected throughout the years. It's my escape from reality, a place where I can let my creativity run wild.

My gaze falls on a pile of fabric swatches next to an incomplete dress. For weeks I've been working on it, hoping to present Harper with a beautiful evening gown for her birthday next month. Clothes are one thing that have really brought us together. She loves clothes and I love creating them from nothing but a few pieces of fabric.

Since I was a kid, it always interested me, the way different fabrics could be transformed into something beautiful and intricate.

The dress I'm making for her is a deep shade of emerald green, with a fitted silk and chiffon bodice. A flowing skirt flares out at the bottom. It's glamorous yet simple, like Harper. I've paid attention to all the details, from the fit and design to the delicate beading and embroidery. And on Harper's birthday, I'll be able to offer her the beautiful gift as a token of our friendship.

I glance down at my phone again, looking at an image I took of her from two days ago. She's standing in the driveway holding the twins' hands, and her hair is pulled back in a low ponytail, revealing a pair of diamond-studded earrings, but the thing my attention is most drawn to is the coat she's wearing.

It's a gray wool coat that reaches down to just above her knees. The fabric appears to be heavy, and the collar is wide, folded down to show off the white fur lining underneath. Silver buttons gleam in the light, and the matching belt cinches the coat at her waist, showing off her curves.

It shouldn't be too hard to recreate it. I'm a talented designer, after all.

Going through the different angles I took of Harper, I carefully examine every crease and stitch in her clothing, committing them to memory so that I can faithfully replicate her outfit. With a practiced eye that only a designer like me can have, I start sketching out the pattern, humming a tune under my breath while adding in the details of the collar and sleeves. All the while my mind begins to race with possibilities for fabrics and trims.

I'll recreate the coat in a different color and slightly different design, adding my own signature touch to it. Maybe a velvet lining instead of fur, or a pop of color on the buttons. Despite the differences, there will be no doubt the two are related, and that's the point. They will be a pair, like Harper and me.

As I sketch, my mind can't help but wander back to thoughts of the nanny. The same questions pop up in my mind. What could her story be? How did she end up here, working for Harper? Is she trustworthy or is she hiding something? There's something about her that makes me uneasy. Maybe it's the way she moves, or the look in her eyes when she doesn't think anyone's watching. Whatever it is, I know I need to find out more.

Without realizing it, my sketch has taken on a more aggressive tone, with each stroke of the pencil pressing harder against the paper.

I set my pencil down and take a deep breath. Maybe I'm overthinking things, getting too paranoid. But with Harper's safety possibly on the line, I can't afford to take any chances.

I take a deep breath and make a decision. I'm going to introduce myself to the nanny. But I need to act natural and make it seem like I'm making small talk, striking up a casual conversation that slowly shifts toward more probing questions.

As I finish my plan of the coat, my phone buzzes with a message from Nolan Jenkins, a simple "goodnight" message.

He's a successful lawyer and we've been seeing each other for a few weeks now. But I've been ignoring his calls for three days, ever since he told me he's thinking of leaving his wife for me.

I ignore the message and put my phone back down on the desk. My focus needs to be on the task at hand. The nanny. Harper's safety. Finding out what's really going on.

THREE

CHRISTA

I flick on the nightlight and stretch my arms above my head, trying to muster up enough energy to get out of bed. As I peer down at Heather inside her cot, my heart swells with love. She's perfect in every way, with her tiny little fingers and toes, and her soft tufts of hair.

Heather's cries had been relentless seconds ago, but as soon as she sees me, her face beams with a smile that could melt the coldest heart. That's why I'm here; that's what makes all this worth it. I instantly feel a deep sense of calm, a renewed sense of purpose and love that only a parent can understand.

"I'm here, my love." As I pick her up, I cradle her in my arms and start swaying back and forth, my hand resting on her back. She giggles and coos, her breath against my neck filling me with warmth.

Heather is a perfect replica of James and me. She has his jet-black hair, and eyes in a shade of blue that seems to change with the light.

My chest constricts when I consider the fact that her father, who's behind bars, will never get to witness this. That's why I'm determined to enjoy our baby for both of us, showering her with all the love she deserves.

A giggle erupts from her lips as I place her on the changing table Harper gave me when we moved into the cottage. It's an expensive custom-made piece of furniture with ornate curves and intricate carvings etched into the pale wood. Most of the baby things she gave me are high-end, things I wouldn't have been able to afford in my wildest dreams.

As I change Heather's diaper while trying to keep her little legs from kicking me over, I glance at the clock on the wall. It reads 2 a.m.

"You're really giving me a run for my money tonight, aren't you, little bean?" Rolling up the dirty diaper and wiping her clean, I smile at her. In response to my comment, Heather's giggles continue to echo through the room while I discard the soiled diaper and replace it with a fresh one.

Once I'm done, I pick my daughter up in my arms and take her to the bed. Cradling her close to my chest, I begin to breast-feed her.

As I listen to her contented murmurs, I find myself slowly dozing off, but soon Heather has had her fill and she has grown drowsy, so I lower her back in the cot.

Instead of going right to bed, I head to the kitchen and make myself a cup of chamomile tea.

The cottage kitchen is cozy, yet quaint. The cupboards are painted a warm yellow and the tile backsplash is a bright white. The appliances are modern, but they fit in perfectly with the rustic charm of the space. I lean against the counter, my warm tea in my hands, and I let out a deep sigh. When I take a sip of the hot liquid, I try to relish the quiet of the night, the safety of this little house. Moonlight filters in through the window, casting a soft glow over the light wooden floor.

I take a deep breath, letting the calming scent of the tea wash over me.

But I can't fully let go knowing that a few steps away in the main house could be the man who might hold the answers that could change my life forever.

Even though I've been watching him closely, I'm still not one hundred percent sure it's really him. The note I received hinted that it was, but I've made mistakes in my past, mistaking someone for someone else. That one error had brought me and others so much heartache that I can't afford to do that again, not with so much on the line.

When I walked through his front door and saw him for the first time, I hoped his response would tell me the truth of who he really is. But it didn't. I've given myself a few weeks to figure it out, and to extract the information I need from him, before I slip off into the night and never have to see his face again.

After standing in the silence for a few minutes, I carry my cup of tea to the living room and make myself comfortable in the surrounding darkness. The dark has a way of wrapping me up like a blanket, sheltering me from whatever comes next—be it tomorrow, next week, or the distant future.

But not long after I sit down, I stand back up and move to the window, pushing it open.

It's too late in the night for any activity on this street. No cars are out and about, and the majority of houses have their lights off, except for the one located across the road.

As I watch Madison's house, my mind swirls with questions about her. Why does she keep watching me? There's always that one nosey neighbor who enjoys prying into everyone else's affairs, but the last thing I need is for someone to be suspicious of me.

I'm not here to win the neighbors' approval, nor am I here to make friends.

The only person I need to befriend is Harper. It's imperative if I want to stay long enough in this place to get what I need. I wonder what she would do if she knew who I really am and that I lied to her to get this job.

I showed up on Troy and Harper's doorstep only a day after their nanny left. What they don't know is that I had something to do with that.

Harper was uncertain about hiring a woman with such a young baby, so I lied.

"It would be wonderful if I could stay home with my baby." I paused for a few seconds before continuing. "But my husband died... a few months ago. He left me with nothing. I need to work to support us. I had to sell our home to pay off some debts."

Harper's face softened with pity and creases of concern formed on her forehead. "I'm so sorry to hear that. So, you're homeless now?"

I nodded sadly, putting on the best performance of a desperate single mother that I could manage. "Yes, we've been staying at a shelter but it's not safe for my baby. I need to get us a place of our own."

I sounded so convincing even to my own ears that I almost believed it myself, sadness creeping into my heart for a moment, like a storm cloud blocking out the sun.

Harper took my contact details and told me she would get in touch.

When days went by without any response from her, I started to lose hope, until she finally called and interviewed me alone, without Troy, as he was out of town. Even though she decided to hire me, she still called my references—though most of them were fabricated.

The calls went out to two students, whom I paid off so they could pretend to be my previous employers, and, of course, they only had great things to say about me.

I close the window again, but continue standing there as I sip my tea. I wonder if other people in the neighborhood are also curious about me. But why should they be? Nannies come and go just like any other job. There's nothing inherently suspicious about it.

The moment I met Harper for the first time, I could tell that she was overwhelmed by the task of taking care of her twin daughters. She appeared disorganized and frazzled as the girls ran around her while their mom attempted to get a word in.

It has only been a week since Harper hired me, but I haven't given her any reason to be disappointed.

I do all the tasks that are assigned to me while balancing the demands of motherhood. The girls are at school during the week, and when they're home, it's all about ensuring they're out of their mother's hair for a few hours, but still close by so she can feel involved. And all of that is easy to do when my baby just wants to be curled up in a sling with me anyway. Plus, they adore my daughter. Two little girls having a baby to stroke and talk to is a godsend.

My daily routine is quite straightforward. The morning begins with me tending to Heather's needs before going to the main house to prepare breakfast for the twins and make sure they are ready for school, unless Harper wants to do it. I then drop the girls off at school and come back home to clean up any mess they left in their wake, and complete any chores that Harper has assigned to me. Since there's also a housekeeper who visits three days a week, I don't have too much cleaning work to do.

While the girls are at school, I'm allowed to take a break to tend to Heather and run my personal errands.

In the afternoon, I pick up the children from school and take them to their after-school activities if needed. In the evenings, I also help out with their homework and see that they are bathed. Afterward, I'm done for the day as Harper or Troy—when he's home—usually take charge of preparing dinner. We agreed that on Saturdays I'd work for half the day, and I'm free on Sundays.

For the past few days, I did my best to surpass Harper's expectations. And now that she knows that she can count on me to do what she's asked, it's time to do what I originally came here for: to talk to Troy.

It has proved pretty much impossible to get him by himself. When he's in the house, he and Harper tend to be inseparable. Part of the reason I'm here is to make sure they can have some private time. When he's not at home, he's at his practice or the local hospital. As a doctor, he works long and irregular hours. Sometimes, he also does volunteer work like Harper.

But I'll find a way to get to him. I have to.

Back in the room, I reach into my bedside drawer and pull out the single white envelope. But I don't open it. Why bother when I already know what's inside: a single name, Troy Wells, and the address of this house.

Attending to the needs and well-being of the children is only one of the reasons why I'm here. Before I can talk to Troy and get any answers, his wife must never find out who I really am, nor anyone else.

I act as if I'm like any other nanny without a secret. But sometimes my thoughts turn toward the person who sent me here. And I wonder, do they have a hidden agenda of their own?

FOUR

Heather smiles as I kiss the tip of her nose. She smells so sweet, like baby powder and the lavender body wash I've had since she first started having baths. I'm the most important person in her universe right now, but sometimes I can't help wondering if she deserves someone better.

I pause when the phone starts to ring, my gaze resting on it as it inches toward the edge of the coffee table. I know who it is; there are not many people who call me, especially at night.

Emily has tried to get ahold of me over the past week, but I've ignored every call. I know she won't be too happy with what I'm doing. But I'll have to speak to her sometime. I can't avoid her forever.

I lift Heather into my arms, and she snuggles up against my neck while I answer the phone.

"Christa! Where have you been? I've been trying to reach you for days." Emily's voice is frantic, and I can tell she's been worried sick about me.

Emily and I have known each other since we were children, living in nearby towns. She's the only person who has ever seen me in my most fragile state. She accepted me for who I am, and never once judged me for my dark past, or the ugly scars it left behind.

Before I left New York, she and her husband and daughter were away, visiting her grandparents in Connecticut. Things had moved so quickly that I hadn't even had the chance to tell her about my plans, which was probably for the best. If I had, she would have tried to talk me out of coming here.

"I'm so sorry, Em." I pull Heather closer, resting my cheek on her soft hair. "I've been busy. When did you get back to New York?"

Emily allows the silence on the other end of the line to extend for a few moments before taking a deep breath. "We returned three days ago and I went to your apartment every day, but you weren't there. I was really worried. Where are you?"

"I'm out of town." I chew a corner of my lip, trying to work out answers to more questions I know will follow.

"Well, that's a good thing. A change of environment will do you good. Where are you guys?"

A vacation would certainly be nice, but, even if I wanted to go away, I don't have money for that.

"I'm in Kentucky. I'm staying with a family over here... working for them."

"Kentucky? What family?" She knows I have no family to visit. "I'm confused. What exactly are you saying?"

"It's a nannying job actually. Sorry I wasn't able to... tell you. It was a last-minute thing."

"What? I thought you didn't want to work as a nanny anymore after—"

"I know, but this is different. I think I've found him, Em." I try to keep my voice steady as I prepare to drop the bombshell on her.

I look down at Heather, who's already falling asleep in my arms.

"Found who?" Emily prompts.

"Brett." I haven't said that name out loud in so long that it feels foreign on my tongue. "Brett Lawson."

There's a sharp intake of breath on the other end of the line, and my heart races as I wait for Emily's response. "What? Christa, are you serious? You're working for Brett Lawson?"

The disbelief is palpable in her words and, even through the phone line, I can feel her shock reverberating around us.

"Yes, him and his wife. They have two kids, twins. I'm their nanny."

"Wait, I'm really confused. How did that happen?"

"When you were away, I got a note in the mail." I let out a long breath. "It's the reason I'm here."

"Right." She clears her throat. "And what did the note say?"

I imagine her rubbing her earlobe, something she sometimes does when she's anxious, worried, or confused.

"It just said to come to this address. There was also a name."

"Let me guess. The name was Brett's?"

"Yes and no. He goes by a different name now, Troy Wells."

"You're kidding me, right? Christa, what are you doing working for that man? I'm sorry but this is a lot to take in."

"The note said I should come to this address." Saying that makes me sound ridiculous even to my own ears. I can only imagine how crazy it all sounds to Emily.

"But you didn't have to listen to that note," Emily presses on, her voice tinged with concern. "You didn't have to go and work for him." She pauses. "So they just randomly needed a nanny and they hired you? Why? He must know who you are."

"He doesn't seem to recognize me... I think. I do look different. I mean it's been a long time and I don't look as malnourished as I did back then." After giving birth to Heather, I craved a fresh start, so I changed up my look, cutting my dark hair to chin length and dyeing it blonde.

Heather stirs in my arms, so I gently rub her back, hoping she'll fall back asleep. "They had a nanny, but she quit."

"She quit, did she? Are you sure you didn't help with that?" Emily speaks slowly, like she's talking to a small child. "What did you say to her?"

"Let's just say I told her a few things that made her want to distance herself from the family and she panicked."

"And that's what you expected her to do, isn't it?" She doesn't sound angry, but I can sense the disappointment in her voice.

"Kind of." Now that the truth is out, there's no point in hiding the rest. I really didn't expect the old nanny to be spooked so quickly but, when it happened, I had to grab the chance. I do feel terrible at times for what I did, but I remind myself why I'm doing this and I push the guilt away.

"I can't believe this. I've been away for only a few days and now you're a live-in nanny for Brett Lawson? How did they even give you a job when you have a baby? And what about Heather?"

"I guess I was lucky. They have a guesthouse and they've allowed Heather to stay with me." Emily is already upset with me. Telling her about the many more lies I told to get here would only make things worse. It's better to keep those details to myself. "Look, Emily, I know it sounds crazy, but I need to do this. You know I do. I can finally find out the truth about what happened."

"Then why not just go ahead and ask him? Why move into his house? Don't you see how crazy this is?"

"I need to be sure it's him. I think it is, but I haven't seen him in years, and he looks very different now. He's not going to just come out and tell me what I want to know. I need to get close to him so it feels he has no choice. If I went up to him on the street, he'd just run away."

"You're not even sure it's Brett?" She lets out a sarcastic laugh. "Oh, great. So you're living with a man who may or may not be who you think he is. That's a brilliant plan. The last time you did something like this it ended badly."

"I didn't... I didn't say it was a brilliant plan," I snap. "But it's the only one I have. Besides, I don't plan on staying long."

"Do you know the person who sent you the note?"

I lean back against the soft cushions and sigh. "No, I don't."

"Do you think it could be Wyatt?" Emily's voice is low and unsure. "Since we don't know where he is, he could be anywhere."

"That's what I keep thinking, but how would he know about Brett?"

The summer before Heather was born, I nannied for a little boy that I wrongly thought was the child that was taken from me when I was younger. And learning the truth came with devastating consequences. Wyatt, the little boy I thought was mine, was not my son. Worse, he was a murderer. I haven't heard from him since the day he revealed to me what he's capable of.

"Frankly, that boy is nuts and I wouldn't put anything past him. He could have done his research. And with all the money his adoptive parents must have left him, he would have the means to hire someone with the expertise needed to find Brett. My question is, what would be his motive?"

I shrug, staring at the closed window. "Who knows? Maybe he wants to help me. We bonded."

"I doubt that very much after everything he's done. If it's really him, Christa, this could be dangerous. Who knows where he is? What if he's close to you?"

I stand up and go to the window, pushing the curtain aside to peer out. "I know, Emily. But I have to take that risk. I need to know the truth. I actually think maybe the person who sent the note wanted to do a kind thing. They know this is what I need."

"I don't know. Something just doesn't feel right about this. I think you should get out of there and come back to New York.

Don't wait until something bad happens. If Wyatt is behind this, it's only a matter of time."

"I can't leave without knowing. I can't leave until I get to talk to Brett. I may not know who sent me here, but this is where I need to be."

"But this might not end well. From what you're telling me, Brett, if it's really him, clearly reinvented himself, going as far as changing his name so he's no longer associated with his past. What if he reacts in a violent way when he finds out who you are?"

"That's another reason why I'm taking it slow."

"I really don't have a good feeling about this." She pauses. "No wonder you didn't tell me. You knew how I would react."

"Yeah, I didn't think you would be on board. But don't worry about me. Everything is going to be all right."

"I'm trying to believe that, honestly. But I'm scared. Please do what you went there for and come back quickly, okay?

I squint to get a better look at the other side of the road, trying to make out any shapes that might be there. Aside from a random car passing by, there isn't much to see.

"I'll be careful, Emily. I promise. And I'll call you as soon as I know something."

FIVE

Two days after talking to Emily, I find myself standing in Troy and Harper's bedroom with Heather strapped to my chest as usual. The entire time I was focused on trying to get Troy alone, but Emily has scared me, made me keen to speed this whole thing up.

I've been wondering if I can prove he's Brett by looking through his belongings. Or if I can find out something about him, his wife, and his new life that I can use as leverage to force him to tell me the truth.

The twins are watching cartoons in the living room downstairs while Troy and Harper are out on a date. Harper called five minutes ago to say they will be home later than expected, as they're going to a movie after dinner, which gives me enough time to have a look around.

Everything is quiet except for Heather snoring softly. The space is beautiful and luxurious with a king-sized bed in the center, fluffy white pillows, and a plush white duvet that looks like it's never been touched.

I haven't been in here before—there's no reason for me to come in here when I'm looking after the girls—but the room is exactly how I pictured it would be: pristine and perfect, just like Harper herself.

The walls are painted in soft pastel colors, and a floor-length mirror reflects the room's peaceful ambience. A dresser made of dark cherry wood stands in the corner, and Harper's makeup is scattered across its top as well as a hairbrush, a bottle of perfume, and various hair products. I scan the items, open the wardrobe, looking for unmarked boxes tucked in secret places.

On one of the bedside tables is a stack of books. One of them has a bright-pink bookmark sticking out of it. I go over to take a closer look, and the title reads *Minimalist Living: A Guide to Simplifying Your Life*. Flipping through the pages, a folded piece of paper falls out and onto the floor. I bend over and pick it up, unfolding it to see what it is.

It's a handwritten letter, and the more I read it, the more my heart drops. It's from Troy to Harper. My stomach churns with unease as I read through the passionate words expressing Troy's love for her. It's clear that they have something real, something that can't be faked or forged.

My lovely wife,

I know I don't say it enough, but you are the light of my life. The way you smile and laugh fills me with such immense joy. I hope to spend the rest of my life making you as happy as you make me, to be able to hold you in my arms and tell you how much I love you. Your smile, your laugh, your touch—they all make me feel so alive. When your fingers dance across my skin, I feel like I'm on fire. You make me want to be a better man, to do things I never thought I could do. I want to be the man who can make all of your dreams come true.

As I take in the words on the page and remember how Troy interacts with his wife in such an affectionate manner, for a moment I have my doubts about him being Brett. How can a man with such a bruised heart and a broken past be able to write such beautiful words, give his heart so completely to someone else?

I fold up the letter again and stick it back into the book.

In the rest of the room, there's no sign of anything out of the ordinary. But sometimes the ordinary can be deceiving. I move to the dresser drawers, rifling through piles of clothes, but find nothing unusual. I even check under the bed, but it's spotless under there as well.

As I scan the space, I notice a picture frame on the nightstand that catches my eye. It's a wedding photo of Troy and Harper. I pick it up and examine it closely. Harper was very young, no older than twenty. My stomach clenches as I lower it back down.

Troy's much younger wife could hint at his identity, but it's not enough. I need more. An old ID with his real name, or maybe a passport, could confirm my suspicions.

If Troy is hiding his true identity from his wife, he would probably not leave any such evidence lying around in their room. Where would someone with something to hide stash their secrets? I need to think outside the box.

I take a deep breath and try to put myself in his head. The truth is, if I were him, I would not leave anything lying around in the house where Harper could find it.

Either way, I walk into the massive closet in case I'm wrong. There could be some secret compartment somewhere.

On one side, there are rows and rows of suits and dress shirts, more than any person could possibly need. Each is perfectly ironed and hung up. As I reach out to touch the clothing, I hear a sound behind me, a soft sigh.

My heart jumps into my throat and I spin around quickly and almost knock over a small table with a lamp on it. Startled, Heather wakes up and starts to whimper.

Madison, the nosey neighbor, stands in the doorway, watching me with a mix of curiosity and suspicion.

"Gosh, you scared me!" I wrap my arms around Heather, trying to keep my tone steady, but my heart is pounding too hard against my ribs.

"What are you doing?" Madison's eyes narrow to slits as she steps closer. "You're not supposed to be in here."

Up until now, I thought Madison and Harper are just friendly neighbors, but they must be closer than I thought if she has a spare key to the house. That's the only way she could have gotten in because the front door was locked. I wouldn't leave it open, not with the children watching TV alone downstairs.

This is bad. Really bad.

I take a deep breath and try to calm my nerves. "I was just... I was tidying up and—"

"I don't believe you." Her voice is sharp, cutting me off. "You were snooping around. I know Troy and Harper hired you as a nanny, not a housekeeper. What are you really up to?"

I hesitate, trying to come up with a believable excuse. But Madison's gaze pierces through me, and I know she won't be easily fooled.

"Actually, the twins were playing in here; it got a bit messy."

She dips her head to one side, never taking her eyes off me. "My friend is one of the kindest and most generous people I know. She has a tendency to trust people easily and always helps people in need." She folds her arms across her chest. "She's done you a favor, letting you look after her children with a baby of your own. I couldn't have done what she did. It's quite peculiar that you turned up out of nowhere. It's not every day that a woman shows up on a doorstep with a baby and asks for a job as a nanny just as the last one left."

My throat tightens and I swallow hard. "I don't understand why you find it strange. Plenty of women work and take care of their babies at the same time."

"Come on, you know what I mean." A sarcastic smile spreads across Madison's lips. "You just conveniently show up when Harper was in desperate need of a nanny? You could be anyone, for all we know. And now you're snooping around their bedroom."

This woman looks like she can see right through me and has the ability to read my secrets. A hot ball of anger rises in my throat, threatening to choke me, but I try to keep my composure. "I assure you, I didn't just 'show up.' I applied for the job like any other candidate, and Harper has my references. She trusts me—"

Thankfully, Heather starts crying louder, interrupting the tense conversation. I take the opportunity to make a hasty retreat, bowing my head as I move to step past Madison. "Excuse me."

She moves into the doorway, blocking my path. "Not so fast, stranger. I know things about you. Things that aren't good."

My stomach lurches but I refuse to show any reaction. She could be lying just to get a response from me. I force a half-smile and gingerly stroke Heather's head to calm her. "I'm sorry, but I don't know what it is you think you know. I'm only here working for Troy and Harper."

"Well, I wonder what they would think if I told them you were snooping around in their bedroom," she challenges me.

It's best not to say anything more as I wouldn't want to dig a deeper grave for myself. Thankfully she steps aside. I don't move for a few seconds, and, when she stays silent, I take that as my cue to leave and quickly step out the door, a sense of unease creeping over me. The nape of my neck prickles as I hurry down the stairs, my thoughts racing.

Not long after, Madison also comes down and walks out of the front door. Will she really tell Harper about my supposed snooping? And what else does she know that she could use against me? What kind of trouble could she stir up?

My insides twisting, I watch from the living room window as she walks back to her house. Suddenly, I feel a tiny hand taking hold of mine and I startle, but it's only Ella, standing next to me, gazing out the window.

"Did Madison come to our house?" she questions me in a quiet voice before continuing without waiting for my response. "She isn't allowed. We don't like her anymore."

I lower the curtain and turn toward Ella, frowning down at her. "What do you mean, sweetheart?"

"Mommy said we're not supposed to talk to her or get any gifts from her."

"Is that so? But she's your mom's friend, isn't she?"

"Nope. They are not friends anymore. She's also not our godmother anymore. We're not allowed to talk to her."

"Do you know why your mom and Madison aren't friends anymore?" I ask, taken aback by this piece of news.

Ella shrugs. "Don't know." Then she slips away from me and goes back to the couch where she continues watching TV.

Confused, I shift my gaze back out the window, but Madison has already gone inside her own house.

If Ella is telling the truth, I'm not the only person who did something wrong tonight. If Madison and Harper are not friends, why does she have a spare key? And what if their brief exchanges in the driveway aren't amicable? Could this be why she never comes inside?

SIX

MADISON

My hand trembles as I slam the door shut behind me and stumble to my living room, collapsing onto the couch. I shouldn't have done that. What had I been thinking? What made me think entering Harper's house with a key she doesn't know I have would end well?

I wanted to talk to the nanny and find out more about her, but when I looked through the window and saw the twins watching TV alone in the living room, I was curious to see what she was up to elsewhere in the house.

Maybe I should have stuck to watching her from a distance. But now that I caught her snooping around, I can't dismiss what I saw. I had a feeling before that she could not be trusted, but to find her in Harper's bedroom, rifling through her stuff, confirms my suspicions.

The question is, what was she looking for?

At least she seems to be unaware that Harper and I are no longer friends. If she does know, she would have said something.

But I can't tell Harper what I saw, not until I have concrete evidence of exactly who the nanny is. I have to find out more.

What if there's nothing to find and you're just being paranoid?

I want to believe the little voice and let go, but I've always had a strong intuition and I sense there's more to find on that woman. I can't deny the negative energy she put off when I got close to her.

She's my chance to get Harper back, but I have to play my cards right and not blow this chance.

My phone rings and I reach into my coat pocket to pull it out. It's my mother again. She probably wants to know when I'm going home to Cincinnati. I haven't gone back in a month and she isn't too thrilled about that. I'm not in the right emotional state to be around my mom, not when she forgets I'm a thirty-year-old adult and continues to treat me like a child.

Since Dad died ten years ago, she formed an unhealthy attachment to me, as if she were afraid of losing me as well. Her endless coddling is suffocating and I need space to breathe. Even worse, whenever she looks at me, she always finds something wrong: my clothes, my hair, my business, my life choices. Nothing is ever good enough for her and it's draining, especially when she keeps on about me finding a husband.

I don't despise my mother. I simply despise the pressure she puts on me to be someone I'm not. She has never forgiven me for choosing to be a fashion designer. She finds it frivolous and unimportant and would have preferred I become a doctor, or a lawyer, like my father was. It's a point of contention between us that we have never been able to resolve. She wasn't even at the opening of my boutique, two years ago.

When the phone doesn't stop ringing, I clench my jaw and force myself to answer it.

"Hey, Mom." I try to sound more cheerful than I feel.

"Madison," my mother says, her smoker's voice thick on the other end of the line. "Yesterday I cooked your favorite meatloaf and mashed potatoes, but you didn't come home for our weekly lunch."

I bite my tongue, trying not to snap at her. "Mom, I told you I wasn't coming."

"Well, you did say you'd consider it," she counters in a tone that's both cajoling and manipulative.

"Yes, I did say I would consider it, but I've been really busy with the boutique lately," I reply, my patience wearing thin. "I sent you a text, remember?"

"That work of yours can wait. Working all the time is not healthy. How do you expect to find a man? It's not like you're saving lives, Madison." There's a long pause on the other end of the line before my mother speaks again. "And you haven't been home for so long. Will you join me for dinner next week then?"

I take a breath and count to three before answering. "Mom, I appreciate your concern, but I'm happy with my life choices right now. Can we please not have this conversation again?"

"But Madison, you're not getting any younger." My mother's tone is turning desperate. "You need to think about settling down before it's too late."

"Too late for what? To be happy?" I interrupt, my voice raising in frustration. "Mom, I'm happy with my life the way it is. I don't need a man to complete me." Crossing my legs, I continue. "In answer to your question, no, I can't come over next week. I was hired to design a wedding dress for an important and high-profile client, and I need to work on it every chance I get. I'm sorry. I'll try to come in a couple of weeks, but I can't make any promises."

Growing up as an only child was not easy. My mom paid so much attention to me that I often wished I had a sister—someone else who could be the focus of her attention. I longed for the kind of connection that comes from having a sibling, someone to talk to late into the night, trade clothes with, and gush about the boys we both liked. So each night, I prayed for a sister.

When I was eleven, my mother put on quite a bit of weight and I thought it meant my wish for a sibling had come true. It didn't matter to me anymore if it was a boy or girl. When I tried to ask Mom about the baby, she became very upset and my aunt Doris explained that she wasn't pregnant. But, in retrospect, as an adult, I sometimes wonder if she lost a baby.

The longing for somebody else to share life with—a person who understood me and with whom I shared my soul—stayed with me all those years. In college, it dawned on me that sisters don't have to be related by blood. I decided I would find a friend who was closer than a sibling.

And I did. Harper.

Siblings fight and they make up. So will Harper and I. We were meant to be together, to be sisters. The moment I met her and introduced myself, I felt it. She is the sister I had been searching for.

She reminded me of Maya, a doll I'd had since I was eight and still do.

The same brown hair that fell in perfect waves around her face and the full, ruby-red lips always turning upwards in a smile that made me feel like I was the most important person in the world.

Maya was my constant companion growing up, a confidante who never judged me.

I can still clearly visualize my childhood bedroom, a princess-themed haven filled with pink and purple accents. And there, sitting on my bed among the fluffy pillows, was Maya, watching me with her big, brown eyes. She was always at the ready for a tea party or a game of dress-up.

The moment I saw Harper, I knew fate had brought us together, that she would become my real-life version of Maya, a friend who wouldn't judge, who would be there for me through everything.

I wasn't surprised when we hit it off right away. We could talk for hours on end.

The first birthday gift I ever bought her was the perfume my mother wore when I was a child, a mixture of rose and vanilla with accents of sandalwood. The same perfume I used to sneak out of my mother's room to spray in Maya's hair when we played dress-up.

Each time Harper wore it, it was like being transported back to my childhood bedroom, with Maya at my side.

My friendship with Harper blossomed quickly, and it was like we had known each other for years.

Everything was perfect. Until the one mistake that ruined it all.

But mistakes happen and mistakes can be undone. When two people are meant to be together, nothing can pull them apart. What I have to do now is fix what's broken, so we can start over. It hurts me deeply the way she looks at me sometimes, like she doesn't recognize me. But she's not unkind. Harper doesn't have one malicious bone in her body. That's why people take advantage of her... people like that nanny.

"You know what, Madison?" my mom breaks through my thoughts. "If you don't come home next week, don't bother coming again." Her voice is sharp, slicing my heart.

"Maybe I won't." I sharpen my tone to match hers.

"Oh, honey." Her tone softens again. "I'm sorry for saying that. I don't mean it, okay? Of course you can come back home... anytime." She pauses. "I don't understand why you won't come and live with me though. We'll have so much fun together like we did when you were little."

I never had fun with my mother because she always ruined it by criticizing me. From the creases in my clothes to the way I tied my hair up, there was always an issue to be addressed. Even when I tidied up my room, it was never good enough for her. There was always something missing, something undone, something that needed fixing, adjusting, or changing. I don't need her or anyone else. The only person who matters to me is Harper. She's the only family I need.

"I need to go, Mom. I have things to do. I'll call you in a few days."

SEVEN

CHRISTA

It's ten to five when I wake up. Even with a baby that keeps me up all night, I still manage to wake early and it puzzles the hell out of me.

When Heather was born, I thought that my days of rising before the sun were behind me, yet here I am, struggling to sleep past five o'clock. No matter how hard I try, my body refuses to forgo habits formed in childhood and forces me awake regardless of whether I'm rested or not, and no matter how late I went to bed.

That's how it always will be, ingrained into me. Habits formed in childhood are hard to break, and this one seems to be rooted down into my very identity. I guess I have to resign myself to a life of never sleeping in like normal people do.

Growing up in a cult, where waking up before dawn to work on the land was mandatory, I suppose it's no surprise that my body still adheres to that strict schedule.

Even though I escaped years ago, my body still won't let me sleep in, as if time has frozen and I am forever stuck in the same morning routine.

My childhood was stolen from me, but I'm here to fix what I

can of my life now. And, to do that, I need to know the truth of what happened to my son.

It's been eleven days since I arrived to work for the Wells family, yet I still can't confirm if Troy is indeed Brett.

There are times I wonder if I'm wrong.

The Brett I remember was tall and skinny, his eyes haunted like those of everyone around him. But Troy doesn't hold much of a resemblance to the person from my past. He has a muscular and toned physique, and his eyes are wide and bright, rather than sunken and hopeless.

There's nothing about him that would make me think he's Brett, but something still keeps nagging at me.

The moment I saw him again when I started working here, I felt something. His mannerisms, his speech intonation, even his walking posture, all reminded me of Brett.

He used to have this habit of tapping his fingers when he was deep in thought. It was a subtle quirk, but it was unmistakably him. And Troy does the exact same thing. Also, his voice, though deeper, has a hint of raspiness that Brett used to have, which is a rare trait.

I remind myself that I'm older and have changed my looks as well, and instead of the dark waist-length hair I used to have, my hair is much shorter and dyed a different color. But it's the little details that can stay the same no matter how much we evolve. I'm surprised he didn't notice. Or maybe he did and he's just too smart or afraid to let it show.

After Madison caught me snooping around Troy and Harper's bedroom, I've been nervous about doing it again, but waiting for a sign to drop into my lap is not going to help. I have to be more careful next time. I'm very lucky that Madison didn't rat me out. At least I don't think she did. But why wouldn't she, though? Unless Ella was right and Madison had no right being inside the house.

I don't want to stay in this house much longer. Waking up

every day and spending time with Harper and her family, when I know I'm here under false pretenses, is starting to eat away at me. I need to find out if Troy is really Brett and leave, for everyone's sake, especially the twins, who I have really grown close to.

I also don't feel safe. That's why Heather is never more than an arm's length away from me, or in a carrier or wrap close to my body. I've lost one child already and I refuse to go through that again.

The room is dark and the blinds are shut, so I can't see Heather, but I can tell she's awake. She makes small chatter in her baby language, like she's conversing with someone only she can see. I'm lucky to have a baby as easy-going as her. When she's fed, changed, and cuddled, she can happily lie inside her cot or on her playmat without crying. She still can't crawl or even roll yet so she's perfectly safe and contained. It makes my job a lot easier.

When I got the job, I promised Harper that having a baby wouldn't get in the way of me caring for her children, and so far I've been able to balance all three kids with no major difficulty —thanks largely to Heather's innate calmness. She's the kind of baby that makes you believe that motherhood is easy.

While she is still happy and before she starts wanting to be fed again, I get out of bed to take a shower. My body feels stiff and tense from all the anxiety and sleepless nights. Still nervous about leaving her alone in the room, I lift her from the cot and bring her with me to the bathroom. I place her in her bouncy chair, making sure the door is locked before getting into the shower cubicle.

The bathroom is cozy in a shabby-chic way, with floral wallpaper and vintage fixtures. It's a welcome change from the modern, sterile bathrooms of most houses these days. Even the showerhead has a slightly rusted look, adding to the charm. To compliment the vintage aesthetic, a small, old-fashioned radio sits on the windowsill, but I don't turn it on today.

I'm humming "The Wheels on the Bus" as I switch on the faucet and the jet of water shoots out from the showerhead and strikes my body. Immediately the sound dies in my throat as the shock of cold hits my system, sending my senses into a frenzy. No matter how many cold showers I take in my life, I'm never really prepared for the initial freezing sensation. The droplets patter against my skin, making me shudder. I stand rigid under the force of the water, feeling its icy rush pelt my skin, plastering my hair to my scalp. I trace a mental path as the water cascades down my face and onto my chin, saturating all of me in a frigid chill. I follow it along the length of my body until it reaches my feet before gurgling its way down the drain.

Allowing the cold to chase away thoughts of discouragement, and doubts that have been swirling in my mind, I try to focus again, to think rationally. Once my body gets accustomed to the cold, I reach out for the bottle of jasmine-scented shower gel on the shelf, squeezing out a generous amount into my palm. The aroma fills my nostrils, calming my nerves as I lather myself up.

As I work the suds all over my body, my thoughts drift to a dark place, but I bring myself back to the present.

The sound of the water pounding against the tiles, Heather's soft cooing, and my own breathing are the only things I concentrate on while the fragrance of the shower gel washes over me, reviving my spirits. My fingers work through my hair, untangling the knots and smoothing out the kinks. The coolness of the water soothes my scalp, and I tilt my head toward the ceiling.

Done with my shower, I wrap a towel around myself, and step out of the cubicle to see Heather grinning at me. A thrill of pride courses through me and I scoop her into my arms.

"Come here, little angel." I nuzzle her neck. In response,

she lets out a giggling coo and buries her face into my shoulder. Inside the bedroom, I open the curtains to let in the early morning light. Together we sit on the bed and watch the world outside awaken to life, like we do on many mornings.

By six, I've fed and changed Heather, and we're heading to the kitchen for me to make myself a cup of tea before getting ready to head to the main house. The second my feet cross the threshold, I spot it—a chessboard sitting in the middle of the kitchen counter.

My throat thickens with panic and I take a step back, still staring at the chess game as if the pieces are about to move themselves.

They stand frozen, the black and white knights facing each other with a menacing air.

Though creepy, it's a beautiful set, made of black, polished wood and delicate ivory. It's not the artistry that makes my heart race, though, but the knowledge of who put it there.

I didn't do it, so someone must have brought it into the cottage.

I feel like at some point I had seen a black and white chess set inside the twins' bedroom while tidying it up, but I can't be one hundred percent sure that it's the exact same set. On closer inspection, I realize that it's not. The pieces are more intricately carved, and the knights are more lifelike, with flowing manes and fierce expressions.

It's not the twins' chess set, and it's certainly not mine. Since leaving Austria, I haven't been able to look at a chessboard or chess pieces without my stomach cramping up, without the memories flooding back along with the horrors attached to them.

The chess set was left there by someone who knows I play.

My thought immediately goes to Wyatt. Chess was the one thing we bonded over in Austria.

My body chills even more than it did under the cold shower as I hurry around the house, checking doors and windows to make sure they're closed and looking to see if anyone is hiding inside. Everything is locked, so whoever came in had a key. I know for a fact there's a spare key in the main house and they could have gotten to it.

Sweat beads on my forehead as I think about what this means, while holding onto Heather tightly, almost suffocating her. Even she notices my agitation and starts squirming in my arms. Gulping in several deep breaths, I reluctantly release her enough to give her room to breathe. It's hard for me to do the same, so I hurry into the living room and sink onto the couch as memories come flooding back to choke me.

If it's really Wyatt who did this, it means he definitely sent the note that brought me here. He's very close and that means everyone around me could be in danger, including Harper and the twins. He's an unpredictable and manipulative kid. There's no knowing what he might do next or how he'll react to any given situation.

But maybe I'm freaking out for no reason. If he really did send me here, he must know that, if I'm going to get what I want, he can't interfere. This could be his way of making things right, proving to me that he has changed. To stop from going insane with worry, I choose to believe that. Perhaps he just wants me to know that he's nearby.

It's still hard to calm my racing heart, but I finally do and I toss the chess game into the bin and prepare for the day ahead.

I'll not let what happened stop me. I've already come so far.

And then another thought creeps in.

There is one other person who might have brought the chess game into my cottage. Someone who taught me how to play my first game of chess.

EIGHT

When I enter the kitchen in the main house, I inhale a deep breath, trying to rein in the anxiety that is taking control of my body, relieved when I see Harper and the twins at the kitchen table. They are a welcome distraction. Harper smiles at me as she fastens a ribbon in Leah's hair, while the girl bites into a peanut butter and jelly sandwich.

"How did you sleep?" Harper asks, her voice soft and gentle.

I shrug, trying to keep my nerves at bay. "Oh, I slept okay. Thanks for asking."

"I'm glad to hear that. By the way, last night I was decluttering the basement and came across a box filled with the twins' baby clothes. Would you like them for Heather? I'm sure she's growing out of her current clothes."

I nod, grateful for the offer. "That's really kind of you, Harper. But you really don't have to. You've done so much for me already."

"I'm not doing it for you," she winks. "I'm doing it for this little angel." She comes close and strokes Heather's cheek. "That face is just too adorable. She deserves the best."

I smile, feeling a warmth spread through me at Harper's kindness toward my daughter.

As Harper finishes with Leah's hair, she hands me a cup of coffee and I take a sip, relishing in the warmth that spreads through me.

"So, what are your plans for today after you drop off the girls?" Harper is already dressed to hit the gym. Black and brown yoga pants hug her curves while a matching sports bra shows off her toned abs. She put her hair up in a ponytail, revealing her defined collarbones.

"Actually, Heather and I will just be hanging out at home today," I say, taking another sip of my coffee. "Maybe we'll watch some movies, read some books. Just some quality time together."

"Sounds like a good plan. You know, sometimes it's the simple things that mean the most." She reaches for a green smoothie and takes a sip, smacking her lips in enjoyment. "Mmm, this is good." She picks up her gym bag, which is already packed and waiting by the door. "Well, I better get going. I have a spin class in thirty minutes."

Going to the gym is her favorite thing to do, when she's not working on her charities in a dedicated office building downtown. She only visits it twice a week, and when she doesn't she either works from home or takes the day off to enjoy other activities that women who don't need to work participate in. Even though she has all the things I wish I could have, I don't resent her for it because she's such a genuine and kind person.

While some wealthy women are involved in charities simply because they want to boast about their philanthropic acts, Harper is different. She seems to truly care about the causes she supports and is always looking for ways to make a positive impact in the world. At least that's how it comes across when she speaks to me about her work.

Two days ago, she became emotional when she told me

about a child she met at a local hospital who was so sick with cancer he couldn't even speak. Since he had no parents, she visited him as often as she could, and it was her hand he was holding when he finally passed away. She was devastated by his loss, but it only made her more committed to her mission. Her letting me work and stay in their house with my baby further proves that she has a good heart.

The day she introduced me to Troy, they laughed when he mentioned that his wife would turn their home into a homeless shelter if she had the chance. Apparently, a year ago, she had brought home a homeless woman and her dog and they'd stayed with them for two weeks.

That woman had been evicted from her apartment and had no family or friends to turn to for help. Harper and Troy housed her, helped her find a job, and even paid her first month's rent in a new apartment.

Deep down I wish Troy is not the man I grew up with, that I'm wrong about all this. I wish I could walk away without disrupting Harper's life.

I want nothing more than to see Troy as a loving husband and devoted father, a good man who supports his wife in all her good deeds. But I cannot because I still think he's someone different, someone Harper might not want to be married to. Someone who did something terrible to me once. And the longer I stay here, the more I realize I might need to protect her, and the girls, too.

Instead of rushing off to the gym as she had wanted to, Harper helps me put the kids in the car. While I focus on the twins, she lowers Heather into her car seat, making funny faces to make her laugh.

"See you later, Harper," I say, getting into the car.

She nods with a smile and peers into the backseat. "Girls, have a good day at school."

We all wave at her as I pull out of the drive. Before driving away, I spot Madison standing in her drive next to her yellow Audi R8, wearing red and black pajamas under a long, black morning robe. She raises her hand to wave at Harper, who doesn't wave back, then wraps her robe around her body and disappears into the house.

Not for the first time I wonder what happened between the two women. I think again about what Ella said—that Madison is no longer their godmother. Harper seems like a forgiving person, so whatever it was must have been quite serious.

The school is only a fifteen minutes' drive away, but it feels longer today as my heart is racing again and sweat has begun to form between my palms and the steering wheel. I keep replaying the events of this morning in my head, wondering what I should do next.

Ten minutes into the drive, the sensation of being watched creeps over me. I glance into the rearview mirror, not exactly sure what or who I'm expecting to see. But Madison's car is behind us. Even though it's a distance away, it's hard to miss because of its bright color. I don't know why, but I've noticed that most people in this town prefer more subtle-colored cars.

At first, I try to shake it off, brushing it off as a coincidence, chalking it up to paranoia. I do my best to keep my cool, but I can feel my anxiety rising. Why is Madison following me? What does she want? My hands start shaking, and I grip the steering wheel tighter.

Maybe she's not following us. It's a small town, after all. She could just be on her way somewhere else.

As we turn onto Main Street, I can see her car still following us in the rearview mirror. She's driving a few cars back, but I can feel her presence looming behind me.

Doing my best to ignore her, I turn my focus to the twins, who are playfully tickling Heather. They love her as much as Harper does, and sadness wells up inside me, knowing that soon they'll have to part with her forever and we will never see them again. I don't want them to feel this pain, but at the same time I know there's nothing I can do. We were never meant to stay here in their lives forever; this was only a temporary stop along our journey.

"Christa, can I feed Heather after school?" Ella asks, but before I can answer, Leah interrupts with a cutting reply.

"That's not fair. I only fed Heather one time yesterday. You did it two times." Her voice is sharp, but the tears around her words are unmistakable. Of the two girls, Leah is the more easily affected one; something as small as a word or gesture can make her cry. Ella on the other hand—I've never seen her cry yet. When she's unhappy, instead of crying she'll become angry and vent on herself or others. It's stunning how twins can be so similar yet so different from each other all at once.

"Don't worry, girls." I glance at them through the rearview mirror, as I try to de-escalate the situation. "Each of you will get to feed her once today, okay?"

Leah mumbles something under her breath, but the argument stops and they seem to calm down, going back to playing with their iPads, which normally stay in the car. I don't condone them being on the iPads the number of times that they are, but who am I to judge? At least most of the things they watch and play are educational, unlike the violent games and movies Wyatt used to occupy himself with.

Fifteen minutes later, I've dropped Ella and Leah off and I'm leaving the school with Heather while a group of kids run past us, yelling and playing tag. The school is large, with a sprawling playground and modern buildings that house classrooms, science labs, and a library. It even has an indoor swimming pool and gymnastics facility, which the twins take full advantage of.

In the parking lot, I get back into the car, but, before I drive off, I scan the area for any sign of Madison. When I don't see her car, I let out a small sigh of relief.

After driving for five minutes I look back in the rearview mirror and, to my horror, I see the car again, in a different lane, but definitely following me. Rage and panic swell up inside of me. This is a really big problem. How in the world am I going to do what I came to this town for when she's standing in my way? What if she blows my cover before I prove Troy's identity?

Instead of driving straight home, I head to the post office to mail the letter I wrote last night to James.

I quickly park the car and get out to rush into the cream building. I take my time inside, wondering if Madison is brave enough to follow me. She doesn't, but, when I return to the parking lot, I see her car parked next to a bakery on the other side of the road. Her head is bent behind a newspaper as she pretends to read, but I know better. What exactly is she hoping to find?

Fed up with her stalking and interference, I walk over to her car with Heather in my arms, feeling my anger boil inside me. When I knock on the window, she jumps in her seat, caught by surprise.

She must have left her house in a hurry because she's still in her pajamas under a coat. Her eyes meet mine and I can see the panic in them, but I don't care. She's pushed me too far. I motion for her to roll down the window and she hesitates for a moment before complying. When she does, I lean down, putting my head inside the car.

"What do you want, Madison?" I hiss, trying to keep my voice under control. "What are you doing following me?"

"Oh, hi there." She forces a smile. "I'm sorry, I don't understand. What makes you think I'm following you?"

"I noticed you earlier when I was dropping the twins off at school. And now here you are."

She straightens out the paper that is resting on her lap. "To be honest, I'm just reading the newspaper, as you can see." Her face betrays her by turning a deep shade of red.

"Ah, I see," I respond coolly. "Have a nice day."

I don't want to worsen the already uncomfortable situation by ruffling her feathers. I need to act like I'm harmless and not arouse any more suspicion in her. Walking away, I can still sense her staring at me, but I don't glance back. I'm hoping that I have shamed her enough that she won't try this again.

NINE

I've been on tenterhooks the last three days, expecting to see more signs that Wyatt is close, watching me, leaving little surprises for me to find. Fortunately, I have not found anything more. I was tempted to ask Harper to change the locks on the cottage, but that could make her suspicious. Instead, I removed the spare key from the main house to keep with me, as an attempt to do *something* to make myself feel better.

Instead of waiting around worrying about Wyatt showing up, or Madison blowing my cover, I have decided that today I will follow Troy.

Heather and I are already dressed and inside the car, waiting for him to drive past. We left the house a few minutes ago and are parked on a corner street a few blocks from the house, so Harper doesn't see me leave the house moments after her husband. As soon as he leaves the driveway, we will follow him wherever he goes.

Last night when I had dinner with them, he mentioned it was his day off today and he planned on meeting up with friends at The Tangerine Club, a place for the rich to meet. It so happens that it's also my day off while Harper is taking the twins to see her grandparents, so I'll have plenty of time to tail him, to watch him, and, perhaps, if need be, to talk to him away from his wife. I might even get an opportunity to see who his friends are. I doubt I'll be allowed inside the club, but maybe they'll meet outside first and I can catch a glimpse of them.

In her car seat, Heather is bouncing with excitement, as if she can sense something big is about to happen. I smile and blow her a kiss. If only she knew how nervous her mother is. My lungs feel like they're filled with lead and one of my legs is shaking uncontrollably. But I can't give up now, not when I'm so close to finding out the truth. I try to take deep breaths and calm my nerves.

Finally, Troy's car drives past, and Heather and I follow at a safe distance, keeping him in our sights as he drives through the winding roads of the town.

We follow him for what feels like forever, until he arrives at The Tangerine Club. But, to my surprise, he doesn't stop at the entrance like I had thought he would. Instead, he continues driving past the club and toward the edge of town, where the buildings become sparse and the roads turn to dirt.

My heart races with every second we follow him. What is he doing out here? Is this where he meets with his friends? Or is he going somewhere else entirely? Did he lie to his wife about where he's going? Maybe he's making a stop somewhere, a quick detour before he heads back to the club. As thoughts swirl in my head, Heather lets out a squeal of delight at something only she knows about and I find myself smiling. But the smile dies on my lips when I glance in the rearview mirror and spot a familiar yellow car.

Madison. Again. What does that woman want from me?

Teeth gritted, I turn my attention back to the black SUV in front of me, wondering where we will end up.

I could turn back now, pretend I'm not tailing Troy, but I can't. I need to know where he's going. It might be hard to talk to him with Madison on my tail, but maybe I'll still get to see something useful.

Pretending that Madison is not behind me, I grip the wheel and follow Troy out of town in the direction of Louisville.

Once we hit the highway, my nerves begin to settle. I keep a good distance between us, making sure to stay in my lane and not attract any attention. Heather falls asleep, lulled by the gentle hum of the car's engine.

I no longer see Madison's car in my rearview mirror, and I breathe a sigh of relief. My focus shifts back to Troy and the mystery of where he's going. Before we reach Louisville, he takes an exit off the highway and heads toward an industrial area, where warehouses and factories dominate the landscape. My heart starts pounding again. What could he be doing here?

Finally, he slows down in front of what at first looks like a nondescript building surrounded by barbwire fencing. But when I look up, I see a sign with a name emblazoned in bold letters—Jefferson County Correctional Facility. I freeze, my foot barely hovering over the gas pedal. What is Troy doing at a prison? My mind races as I try to piece together the puzzle. Is he meeting someone here? A friend or relative perhaps? The possibilities are endless and my curiosity is piqued.

The building is gray and foreboding, with tiny windows, its concrete exterior giving off a sense of unease. My heart races with a mix of fear and confusion.

My mind reels with questions as I park the car as far away from the prison gates as possible. I wouldn't want the cops to ask me what I'm doing here. Troy, on the other hand, drives up to the gate and a few seconds later he drives right through it.

This could be the sign I had been waiting for, proof that he might be leading a double life. Proof that he's not who he says he is. Troy's secret visit to the prison could mean anything. If Harper doesn't know about him being here, I could use his lies to get what I want.

I take a deep breath and get out of the car, trying to act as casual as possible. My eyes dart around, taking in the sights and sounds of the prison. Guards patrol the perimeter, their focus on the visitors. The air is chilly and thick with the smell of concrete and iron, and sounds of clanging gates and barking dogs echo in the background.

I hesitate for a moment, unsure of what to do. Should I stay here and wait for him to come out? Am I even allowed to be here? I'm not a visitor, nor am I authorized personnel. Who knows how long Troy will be inside?

After waiting for fifteen minutes, pacing around the car with my gaze directed to the entrance, a guard approaches me, his stern expression telling me that he's suspicious of my presence. He's broad and imposing, his uniform crisp and neat. As he draws closer, his jaw tightens, and his gaze moves from me to the car and back.

"Can I help you, ma'am?" His hand moves to rest on his gun.

I swallow hard, my palms sweating. "I'm waiting for someone," I reply shakily, knowing full well that my answer won't suffice.

"Anyone specific?" he presses.

I try to keep my composure, but my heart picks up pace. My mind is blank, searching for the right words to say. Finally, I manage to stammer, "Yes, my husband. He's visiting a friend inside." I try to sound as convincing as possible.

The guard furrows his brow, clearly not convinced by my explanation. "I'll need to see some identification."

I don't want him to know my name. What if Troy finds out that I came here? I glance around, looking for an excuse to leave. My gaze goes to Heather in the car. She's no longer sleeping but awake, stretching her arms out in front of her.

"Ma'am, I need to see your identification," the guard repeats impatiently.

"I don't have it on me. I left it at home." I normally don't carry my ID, but he could ask for my driver's license, and that also has my name on it. I need to get out of this, so I point to Heather through the windshield. "You know what, I won't wait for my husband after all. My baby is tired, and I should get her home."

The guard studies me for a moment, his lips pursed, and finally nods. "Very well, ma'am. I suggest you leave now, as this is a restricted area."

"Thank you." I quickly get into the driver's seat and start the car, relieved to leave the compound without incident. As I pull away, I glance back at the guardhouse in the rearview mirror. The guard is still standing there, watching me go. My mind races as I try to figure out what to do next. I drive aimlessly for a while, trying to calm down and think clearly. In the end, I decide to head home since Heather is due for her nap and a feeding. I'll find another way to get to Troy, and soon.

Troy doesn't come home until dinnertime. He finds me, Harper, the twins, and Heather eating spaghetti and meatballs at the kitchen table over candlelight.

When the twins are particularly energetic, Harper sometimes resorts to using the candles as a calming technique. The cream candles in silver candlesticks cast a warm glow across the room, making everything seem softer, kinder.

I look up from my plate as Troy enters the room, his face etched with exhaustion and dry sweat stains peeking out from his armpits. When he smiles, his teeth glint in the candlelight. But there's a weariness behind the gesture that I can't ignore. When he reaches the table, Harper kisses him on the lips then cups his face with both hands.

"You look exhausted, my love. Was it draining at the prison?"

Disappointment fills me as I realize that Harper knew where Troy was today. And here I was thinking he was keeping a secret from her.

"It was exhausting, to be honest." Troy moves on to kiss his daughters, then he drops into a chair opposite to mine. "Hi, Christa, did you have a good day off?"

Are his eyes lingering on my face for a little too long or am I imagining things? What if he knows I followed him? I try not to let my thoughts show on my face. "Yes, it was all right. I was out and about with Heather."

"Good. As you already heard, I spent most of the day behind bars." He laughs out loud.

"Don't be silly." Harper swats him on the arm and explains what he means. "Once or twice a month, Troy visits prisons to offer his medical services." Harper squeezes her husband's arm. "He's as much of a softy as I am." She pauses to look at her husband. "But I wish he would take more time off. The man never stops working. I was hoping today he would at least slow down a little and make time for himself."

Troy nods in agreement. "I know, I know, honey. I promise to do that next time." He picks up a fork and starts eating the food Harper has scooped onto his plate. "There were several emergencies today and there are not enough medical professionals lining up to help inmates."

I watch the conversation between them, my stomach clenching with nerves. Could it be that I'm assuming too much? Perhaps Troy really is who he says he is after all.

TEN

MADISON

I clutch the mug tightly, the aroma of chai tea drifting into my nostrils. Through the kitchen window, I watch Troy and Harper eating breakfast with Christa. Harper tilts her head back, laughing at some joke without knowing the danger she is in, of the snake sitting next to her.

When I saw Christa following Troy yesterday, it suddenly hit me that there must be something going on between the two of them, and I was sure they were headed to some secret location where they could enjoy each other's company without anyone else around. I would have loved to see where they ended up if it weren't for that fender bender that had spoiled my plans. A jerk in a red sedan had rear-ended my car, causing me to swerve off the road and lose sight of Christa and Troy's cars.

But what I had seen was enough for alarm bells to go off in my head.

I finish my tea and pull up my binoculars from the kitchen counter. I focus in on Troy and Christa's faces. They're trying to act normal around Harper, pretending that nothing is out of the ordinary. But I can see the guilt etched in their expressions.

I need to find a way to tell Harper what's going on before

it's too late. But I need to do it without raising any suspicions from Troy and Christa. I can't let them know I'm on to them.

I wait until Christa leaves to take the kids to school and Troy goes to his practice. I need time to talk to Harper alone with no distractions.

Half an hour passes before that happens, the longest time of my life.

As soon as the two cars disappear down the road, I grab my coat and head out the door. I'm in such a rush that I almost forget the keys in the lock, which would have shut me out had I not remembered.

"Silly girl," I mumble to myself as I reach behind the door to pull them out. Doing something like that wouldn't be smart, especially since Harper no longer has my spare key, even though I had made a copy of hers before giving it back.

I catch her as she's leaving the house, dressed in workout clothes under a camel coat. A yoga mat is tucked securely under her arm while she holds a glass bottle of water in her other hand. I approach as she's locking the door, and, when she turns around, she startles and drops the yoga mat. The water bottle slips from her hand, shattering on the ground below. Water splashes onto the concrete, and she jumps back, startled.

"Why are you sneaking up behind me like that, Madison?" She throws her hands into the air before they fall back at her sides. "Look what you did."

"I'm so sorry, Harper. I didn't mean to startle you." I bend down to pick up some of the larger shards of glass. "Let me help you."

"I'll handle it," Harper snaps as she unlocks the door again. She marches back into the house, muttering something under her breath.

"No," I persist, trailing behind her. "Please let me help. It was all my fault and I feel terrible about it. I'm really sorry."

Standing in front of the kitchen door, she whips around to

face me. "I need you to leave." Her voice is both cold and brittle. "You're no longer welcome here, remember?" Her words are meant to intimidate me into leaving, to send me packing with my tail between my legs. But even when she's angry, she looks adorable—her freckles darkening and her dimples deepening as her nose turns bright red.

Instead of being offended, I want to hug her, to comfort her. The woman doesn't have a single evil bone in her body.

Before saying anything else, I walk past her and toss the shards of glass into the bin.

"I said get out of my house, Madison," Harper repeats, her hands on her hips now, still not threatening, still just as adorable.

"I wanted to talk to you, that's all. That's why I came over." I try to reach out to her, but she takes a step back.

I tuck a lock of hair behind my ear and let out a sigh. "I came here to warn you about something."

"Warn me about what exactly?" She folds her arms across her chest.

"You can't trust Christa. I think she has an agenda."

Shaking her head, Harper enters the kitchen and reaches for a broom from behind the door, along with a dustpan. But, before she leaves the room, I grab her by the shoulders and turn her to face me.

"Harper, I know I did something wrong. I hurt you. But I didn't know what I was doing. I was drunk and it will never happen again. It was Troy who—"

"Drunk or not, you made a choice, Madison," Harper interrupts me, her voice firm. "And that choice has consequences."

I take a breath and change direction. "I know you hate me right now, but the woman caring for your kids is a more serious threat than me. I think she's here for a reason and it has nothing to do with the job you hired her to do." I let my words sink in before continuing, praying that she won't leave before hearing me out. "I think she's having an affair with Troy."

"How dare you make such an accusation! Not everyone is like you." Harper's eyes widen with shock and anger, and this time the cuteness is replaced by a fiery intensity. Without another word, she goes back outside to clean up the mess I made. As she bends down to pick up more shards of glass, I see her finger brush against a jagged edge—and a bead of blood wells up on its tip. She puts her injured finger in her mouth for a few seconds before continuing to tidy up as if nothing had happened.

Without thinking, I rush back into the house and open a kitchen drawer I know is filled with Band-Aids. In the past, when I was allowed to babysit the twins, they loved the various characters and sweet designs on them. They constantly found excuses to wear one even when they were not hurt. The superhero and princess Band-Aids were their favorites.

I loved spending time with the girls and treated them like my own. By distancing herself from me, Harper has also robbed me of the opportunity to be a part of their lives, to watch over them. I never want children of my own, but if anything ever happened to Harper and Troy, I would take care of the twins in a heartbeat, and would never let anything harm them. As their godmother, I've always felt a sense of responsibility toward them, a duty to protect them from any harm. I used to love referring to them as "my girls."

The day Harper asked me to be the twins' godmother was special. We were sitting in their backyard, drinking lemonade in the hot summer sun. The twins were two weeks old and lying in their bassinets beside us, their tiny hands and feet moving in the air.

"Madison, I can't think of anyone else I trust more with my babies," Harper said, her voice soft and sincere. "If anything happened to me or Troy, I know you would take care of them like they were your own."

My heart swelled with happiness as I nodded, feeling honored and proud. I was touched by her words and I knew that being a godmother was a responsibility I would take seriously.

I love the girls almost as much as I love their mother, and I want to be able to hug them again, and to spoil them with their favorite gifts. Every time I come across something I think they might like, I still buy it, wrap it up, and keep it in my basement in the hopes that one day I'll be allowed to hand the gifts over.

I shake my head to clear my thoughts, and grab a Band-Aid with a cartoon dinosaur, before making my way back to Harper. "Here"—I offer it to her—"Let me help you."

Harper looks at me skeptically, but, after a moment of hesitation, she allows me to take her hand and apply the Band-Aid to her cut.

She doesn't say anything else or ask me to leave again as we finish cleaning up. When we're done and she's ready to go back into the house, she looks me straight into the eye.

"Madison," she says finally, "Christa is a wonderful person. She came here because she needed help, and so did I. Linda quit without warning and I needed someone to fill in."

"But don't you find it strange that she appeared out of nowhere, before you even put up an ad?"

She shrugs. "Maybe it was a miracle."

Harper is a religious person and she never once misses church, going every Sunday, taking the kids. I find it weird that Troy never accompanies her.

"I don't want to watch you get hurt." My voice is low and serious. "I really care about you. And I don't trust her. Please believe me."

"It's not your responsibility to worry about me... not anymore. We used to be friends once, but we no longer are. I need you to respect that."

She stands up and walks back inside, this time closing the door behind her. I stay outside for a few minutes and, when she doesn't come out, I return to my place. But I'm not going to give up that easily.

Harper walks through the front door again about fifteen minutes later, and as soon as she has driven off, and nobody's watching, I go back to their house, walking past the main building on my way to the cottage. The door is locked, but that's not a problem.

Growing up, I was really good at breaking into homes and cars. It was something my friends and I did for fun. There was no place I couldn't get into.

I had no need to steal because my parents had the money and could afford to get me whatever I needed, but I guess I craved the adrenaline rush that came with the danger of being caught. It also brought me satisfaction to prove to my mother that I wasn't the perfect little girl she wanted me to be.

I run back to my house and return with a hairpin. The kitchen door is an old-fashioned wooden door and it wouldn't be hard to jimmy the lock. I make quick work of the lock with my tool, my fingers moving with deft precision. Fortunately, the rear of the home is not visible from the road, so I'm safe from prying eyes.

Once I'm inside, I head straight for the bedroom. The scent in the room is a strange combination of musk and lavender perfume.

The space is neat, organized, and the bed is made to perfection. The pillows, which are neatly stacked against the headboard, are fluffed and there's not a crease on the crisp white sheets. A red quilt lies folded at the foot of the bed.

The empty baby's cot next to the bed catches my attention. It's one of the cots that had belonged to Harper's kids. Why would she give a stranger something so personal? I shake off the thoughts and focus on my mission. I go through the dresser drawers, looking for anything that will give me a clue about the nanny and her life, anything that I can use to my advantage.

In the closet, I come across a handbag hanging on a hook. It's a battered old thing, brown leather frayed and stained in some places. I open it and begin rifling through its contents. There's a wallet, some loose change, clear lip gloss, and several receipts. I study the receipts but find nothing of importance.

What I do find strange is that, aside from the handbag, there are no clothes hung up or folded, which means she has not unpacked, which is unusual as she's been here for two weeks. It's almost as if she's not planning to stay. I need to find the suitcase and see what's in there.

After looking around for it, I find it under the bed, hidden in a corner. I pull it out, taking care not to make too much noise. It's a small, black suitcase, and I wonder how long Christa is planning to stay if that's all she brought with her. I unzip it and find a couple of pants, t-shirts, underwear, and toiletries.

I'm not surprised that all her clothes are black. I've never seen her wear any other color. That was the first thing that made her seem strange to me. I make sure to check every pocket and compartment, and that's when I find it. An envelope, tucked away in the inner pocket of the suitcase.

My heart races as I pull it out, eager to find out what secrets it holds. The name on the front is Christa Rogers along with an address in New York. Having her full name is a great start to finding out everything else about her.

I hesitate for a brief moment, considering if I should open the envelope or not. But I know that this could be my only chance to find out more about Christa, to prove she's not who Harper thinks she is.

It's a typed note, and as I read it, my suspicions are confirmed.

What you're looking for is here is written on one line,

followed by a name and address below it. Troy and Harper's home address.

Holding the paper between my fingers, my heart beats faster and harder. This is it. This is what I'm looking for. Maybe I was wrong in thinking Christa is having an affair with Troy. But this note proves she's up to something, that she moved into their home for a reason.

I quickly take a photo of the note, but, before I can put my phone away, I discover a passport tucked away in another pocket and snap a picture of the details page.

Glad I found something, I carefully tuck the note and the passport back in the suitcase and slip out of the cottage, knowing exactly who I need to ring to find out the truth.

ELEVEN

CHRISTA

Troy and Harper are downstairs preparing dinner together, and I'm helping the twins with their bath, while Heather is in her bouncer chair next to the tub, playing with a black and white rattle. Bubbles fill the air as Leah and Ella giggle and splash around in the water.

When I leave, I'll miss the twins, especially their laughter. I don't know why I always have to get attached so much. Last time it got me into a whole lot of trouble and here I am still doing it.

"You're next, Ella." I reach for the sweet-scented shampoo, turning to the little girl. As I pour the shampoo onto her hair, my mind drifts away. Since following Troy and coming up with nothing, I've been doubting myself and what I'm doing. The longer I stay, the more I care about Harper, and I've found nothing of substance to prove that Troy is Brett.

As the kids blow bubbles at each other, my heart aches to think I could be here for nothing, that I wasted my time following a lead that could very well have reached a dead end. But still there's that little fire burning in the pit of my stomach.

It may be faint now, but it's there, glowing with determination, reminding me to keep pushing forward.

Last night, I decided I'll give it another few days and, if I find nothing, I'll leave.

"Dinner's ready," Harper calls from downstairs.

"We're almost done." I snap out of my thoughts and quickly rinse out Ella's hair before helping her out of the tub.

It takes another fifteen minutes for the girls to get dressed and we all head downstairs to the inviting aroma of roasted meat and steaming vegetables. Troy and Harper have set out the dishes on the table.

"Christa, you're staying to eat with us, aren't you? As always, there's a plate here with your name on it." Harper points to a beautiful antique plate at the seat beside her.

"Sure. But if you don't mind, I'd like to go and feed Heather first."

"Of course, take all the time you need. We'll save your seat," Harper replies with a warm smile. "Use the living room if you like."

I'd rather breastfeed Heather in the privacy of our cottage, so I decline and tell them I won't be long.

Feeding Heather, I try to shake off feelings of unease, focusing on the present moment, savoring my time with my daughter as she nurses contentedly. Her little hand grabs onto my shirt, and I feel a sense of peace in her gentle presence. After burping her, I make my way back to the main house and take the seat next to Harper.

A few minutes into dinner, I don't notice that I'm not eating until Harper points to my plate.

"Are you all right, Christa?" She reaches out to take my hand, but I jerk away reflexively.

She gives me a wounded expression before I smile and assure her that I'm all right. "I'm sorry. I was lost in thought."

"You're thinking about your husband, aren't you?" Her voice is so gentle and supportive that my heart swells.

I nod, feeling the lump forming in my throat. "Yes, I miss him terribly."

Troy clears his throat, bringing everyone's attention to him. "What happened to your husband? How did he..." he glances at his daughters "... actually, it's not important. You don't need to talk about it. We're really sorry for your loss."

"Thank you." My gaze locks with his until he's the first to look away.

"It's understandable that you will have some low days," Harper continues. "When you lose a loved one, you never fully heal, I think. People keep saying time heals all wounds, but I don't believe it." She presses a napkin to her lips. "I'm not sure whether I told you this, but I was a twin."

"Really?" I lean forward, interested in finding out more about her. "No, I didn't know that."

"My sister, Lila, died when I was sixteen." She blinks several times before dropping her gaze to her food.

"I'm so sorry to hear that." My heart goes out to her. It already hurts to lose someone you love, but losing someone that close must be devastating. I don't ask how she died because I feel that would be too intrusive of me. I wouldn't want her to hurt more than she already is. Instead, I try to offer comfort. "It must have been really hard for you."

"It was." She looks up again and gives me a sad smile. "But things got easier with time. I've learned to live with just her memory."

I nod and gaze out through the massive window at the lake lining the property, watching the water sparkling in the evening light.

"It's a beauty, isn't it?" Harper says finally when I look back at her. Troy has his arms around her shoulders now.

"What?" I ask, surprised.

"The boat." Harper points to the window. "Isn't it beautiful?"

"Yes." I look out again, watching the boat sway gently in the wind, and I wonder if they use it often. "It's really beautiful."

The boat is a sleek, white motor yacht, with a long bow and a spacious deck. I can imagine how nice it would be to take it out on the lake, watching the sunset as the water laps gently against the hull.

"Maybe we can take it out for a ride sometime." Harper seems to read my thoughts.

"Oh, no." I shake my head. "Unfortunately, I have a terrible fear of being on boats. I prefer to admire them from a distance."

"Why is that?" Troy asks, his fork halfway to his lips.

"I... umm... it's embarrassing, but I have this fear that the boat would capsize and... well, I can't swim."

"You can't?" Harper is shocked. "You never had the opportunity to learn?"

"No, I didn't." As I speak, I glance at Troy to see if he has a reaction to my admission, but he simply nods sympathetically. "And I don't feel the need to learn now. I'm perfectly content to stay on dry land."

Harper shifts her chair closer to the table, watching me intently. "Did something happen in your childhood that made you afraid of boats and water?"

"Yes. When I was a child, I managed to get onto a dingy little boat and it capsized, leaving me stuck under the water for what felt like forever. I almost drowned. Since then, I decided I would never step into a river or lake again. The shore is the farthest I would go. I do enjoy watching bodies of water as long as I'm not in them." I look again at Troy quietly eating his dinner.

Harper squeezes my hand. "Don't worry, there's nothing embarrassing about it."

After dinner, I offer to wash up while Heather and the

twins play with Harper in the living room. Troy excuses himself to make some calls and, finally, I'm ready to retreat to my cottage.

Heather and I are making our way down the path when I hear someone speaking from the back of the house, hidden from view. Cautiously, I make my way toward the voice, my curiosity getting the better of me. As I round the corner, I see Troy pacing back and forth, a troubled expression etched on his face. His phone is pressed to his ear as he tugs at his hair in frustration.

Fortunately Heather is quiet, sucking on her fingers.

"I can't," Troy says through gritted teeth. "You need to stop calling me when I'm home with my family."

I step back, my mind spinning, wondering who he's talking to, wishing I could hear what the person on the other end is saying.

"Drew," he growls, "I know you're my brother, but, like I said, it's too risky for me to come again so soon. I'll send what you need, but don't you ever call me at home again. That's an order. I will call you."

When Heather starts fussing, afraid she might cry, I make a beeline for my cottage and close the door behind me. After putting her on her playmat with her teething ring, I dig through my purse for the phone and dial Emily's number, barely able to contain my racing thoughts.

"It's him. Oh my God, it's really him," I say as soon as she picks up.

"Did you find something to make you believe that?" Emily sounds excited on the other end.

"I overheard him on the phone with someone he addressed as his brother, Drew. Em, Brett's younger brother was Drew. It has to be him."

Adrenaline rushes through me and dizziness makes my world spin, like I'm on a roller coaster hurtling toward the unknown. The room suddenly feels too small and I'm desperate to get out. Taking deep breaths, I steady myself against the wall, but my body is shaking uncontrollably.

Emily is silent on the other end for a moment, likely processing the information.

"Oh my God!" she mutters finally. "It's really him?" Even though the line is crackling with static, I can hear the excitement in her voice.

"Yes, it is." My mouth is dry, my throat tight as though I've swallowed a handful of sand.

"So you were right all along. How do you feel?"

"To be honest, I feel sick to my core." I wrap an arm around my stomach as an intense feeling of nausea rises swift and strong like an ocean. "I'm suddenly not sure what to do next. I wasn't prepared for this."

I thought I was ready to confront him, but now that it's confirmed that Troy is Brett, I'm not sure how to feel.

The excitement is there, sure, but it's mingled with a sense of dread that I can't shake. My entire body feels hot and cold at the same time, like I'm burning up while simultaneously freezing over.

"Honey, you don't have to do anything right this minute," Emily says, her voice calming. "Just take a deep breath and try to relax. We'll figure out the next step together."

When Heather makes a cooing sound, I shift my gaze to her, but my vision is blurred with tears. I wipe them away and take a deep breath as Emily's words sink in. She's right, I don't have to do anything now. I can take my time, plan my next move carefully. But there's no time to waste.

"I need to speak to him soon. Harper is going away for a retreat this coming weekend. I'll use the time to talk to him while we're alone in the house." It would certainly be less complicated without his wife there to possibly overhear our conversation.

"Okay, that's a good opportunity. But Christa, you need to be careful. You have no idea how he might react. You have to be prepared for anything." Emily lets out a loud sigh. "Are you really sure you want to go ahead with this? I'm scared for you."

"I know, but I need to do this. I need closure," I reply with determination in my voice. "And knowing that Troy was hiding that phone call from Harper kind of gives me some leverage I can use against him."

"Yeah, you're right. But please be safe, okay?"

"I will."

We end the call and I sit there for a moment, staring at the phone in my hand.

The thought of confronting Brett is both exhilarating and terrifying.

What if, in order to protect his new identity, he lashes out and hurts me in some way? I shake my head, trying to push away the negative thoughts. I can't give in to fear. I've come too far to back down now.

TWELVE

The Cedar Lane Playground is bustling with activity, filled with the roars of excited children, who are high on the adrenaline that comes with being young and carefree.

Parents and guardians sit lazily on nearby park benches, reading, talking to other parents, or glued to their phones. The swings creak as they're pushed back and forth, the slide squeaks as each child comes down, and the jungle gym echoes with the sound of little feet running on it.

I'm sitting on the bench with Heather's stroller next to me, close to a large sandbox. Leah and Ella are jumping up and down in it, their laughter blending with the noise of the playground. I watch them, amazed at how carefree and full of energy they are.

As soon as I took them home after school, Harper asked me to bring them to the playground as she was in full baking mode for a charity event at the club tomorrow. I understood why she wanted them off her hands. Leah was not giving her a moment to prepare. She's so clingy at the moment because she knows her mother will be going away on Friday, and it's already Wednesday. Yesterday, she cried bitterly about not wanting Harper to go.

I was happy to spend more time with the girls, especially since the clock is ticking until the time when I'll have to part with them.

As I burp Heather on my shoulder, I think about Harper. She was different yesterday, not her usual self at all. She barely said a word to me, and, at dinner time, she asked me politely if I would mind eating by myself in the cottage as she wanted to spend some much-needed time with the twins before she left for her retreat. It would be just the three of them because Brett had a late night at the hospital. Of course, I gave them their space and ate on the couch in the cottage, watching reruns of *Cheers* while encouraging Heather to practice rolling over on the carpet at my feet.

But my thoughts kept drifting to Harper and what could be bothering her. Even today she was not her normal happy self, and barely cracked a smile. Maybe it's one of those moments, the low ones that everyone gets from time to time. But what if it's more than that? A small part of me wonders if she knows who I am or what her husband is hiding.

And I'm more worried for her and the girls than I was before, having searched online for information on Drew. A quick search revealed that he's currently incarcerated in the exact same prison that Brett visited, for being intimate with underage girls. Maybe someone else would have been shocked by this, but not me, not after what I know about the dark past they're connected to.

As much as I'm ready to confront Brett, I'm also nervous of what his reaction will be to discover that his cover has been blown, and his carefully constructed life could come crashing down. When people feel like their lives or livelihoods are threatened, there's no knowing if they will act like a cornered animal, or whether they will strike.

I'm still in my thoughts when, from the corner of my eye, I notice someone coming to sit next to me. It's probably a parent watching their kids play, but I can't be bothered to look.

Then I hear a voice, a simple hello that sends a shower of cold dread pouring down my back.

My head snaps back, and I almost drop Heather in shock.

"Hi, Christa," Wyatt sneers at me. "Did you miss me?" His voice is laden with an ominous tone that makes my stomach clench up.

The terror I felt the day I saw him in front of the school in Cove Haven, when he confessed to murdering his previous nanny, comes rushing back to me with a force that almost knocks me out. I did expect that he might show up ever since the chessboard I found in the kitchen, and feared it was him that sent me the note, but I still hoped I was wrong, that it was someone who's less dangerous than the sixteen-year-old sitting next to me.

He looks different from when I last saw him. His honey-colored hair almost touches his shoulders as it spills out of a black baseball cap, and he's wearing a white t-shirt with a picture of a horse across the front. I peel my gaze from the horse, which brings up too many painful memories, and focus on his face, my gaze tracing the hard edges of his jawline. He's still a boy, but doesn't look like one at all to me, not anymore.

"What do you want, Wyatt?" I try to keep my voice steady, but it wavers a little as I get to my feet.

"I thought you would be happy to see me. But at least I'm glad you got the note I sent you and knew what to do." He removes his cap and places it on his knee. "I wasn't sure whether you would take the bait."

"You should leave before I scream." My voice is trembling with fear and I'm sure he can hear it.

"Aw, don't be like that, Christa. Since you came to see me

that day, I did a lot of thinking, and I want us to be a family." He sighs and runs a hand through his hair. "You're my mother. We deserve to be together."

My heart jumps to my throat as I shake my head. "Wyatt, we're not related. I'm not... I'm not your mother. We did a DNA test, remember?" I hold my own baby tighter, as if he would snatch her from my arms and disappear just to cause me pain.

"I don't believe the stupid test." He wrings his cap between his hands so tightly his knuckles turn white. "What matters is how I feel. I know you're my mother and now I have found my father. I was waiting for you to confirm it's him. That's why I waited before I showed up. Now that I know—"

"How?" My knees feel faint as though I'm about to drop to the ground. "How do you—"

"How do I know you figured it out?" He chuckles and releases his grip on the cap. "Let's just say I have my ways."

My throat goes dry. The only way he can know is if he heard me talking about it. The only person I talked to was Emily on the phone, and since she wouldn't have spoken to him, he must have listened in on my conversation, which means he was close enough to hear. Was he inside my cottage? My stomach lurches, pushing bile up my throat.

Wyatt moves closer. I flinch when he lays a hand on Heather's head, stroking her hair. "Hi there, little sister," he murmurs. "It's nice to meet you up close. I can't wait to babysit you."

I take a step back and he removes his hand, grinning. "She's cute, and she looks like James. Does he know he's a father?"

"I need you to leave us alone." My voice trembles as I look around, maybe for the police. "Don't ever come near me or my baby again."

"You can't push me away. I love you and I know you love

me. I saw it in your eyes from the day we met. I heard it in your voice."

"That was before—"

"Before you knew what I did?" He raises an eyebrow. "But you're my mother. You should be able to forgive me for anything."

"I already told you I'm not your mother." I blink away the moisture from my eyes as I meet his gaze head on. "Wyatt, I really wish I knew where your mother is. I did wish it was me, but it's not. I'm so sorry."

"You *are* my mother." His voice is softer now, deeper. "And if you don't accept that we're a family, I don't know what I might do."

Instead of responding to him, I call for the girls. We cannot return home until I get a call from Harper, but I'll find someplace else for them to play.

"I'll leave." He raises his hands, palms facing outwards. "But I'll be back. When I return, I need to know that you accept me as your son. And don't do anything stupid like calling the police, or something bad might happen." Before I can stop him, he approaches me and wraps his arms around my body in a hug, then he steps back and kisses Heather on the forehead. He gives me a wink before walking away, his hands in his pockets.

As soon as he leaves, I sink back onto the bench, my entire body trembling. Someone touches my shoulder and I flinch, turning to see an older woman with gray hair looking kindly at me.

"Are you okay, sweetheart?" The concern in her voice is audible.

"Yes." I wipe the wetness from my cheek with the back of my hand. "I'm a little faint, that's all."

"Here, drink some of this." She hands me a small bottle of water and I thank her. But as I reach for it, it falls to the floor.

She picks it up again and opens it before handing it back to me. "You'll feel better."

Feel better? I don't think I will ever feel better. I don't think I'll ever have a normal, calm life. Not as long as Wyatt believes we're meant to be together. I know the extent of his obsession, and now I'm his target. He will not stop until he gets what he wants. And it's all my fault. I'm the one who stalked him first.

THIRTEEN

I'm still shaking when the kids and I get into the car and drive away from the playground, with me constantly checking the rearview mirror. Seeing Wyatt has changed everything. It's made me realize how much danger I'm putting everyone around me in. I know I cannot wait until tomorrow to speak to Brett. I need to do it today. Hopefully, he won't be working late.

Tomorrow, after dropping the twins off at school, I'll leave. I'll already have my bags packed and loaded into the car so that I don't have to return.

I need to get the truth out of Brett before I leave town. I need him to tell me where my son is, so I can find him and keep him with me.

Shortly before six we arrive at the house. As soon as I open the door, we're immediately met by the smell of baking. The sweet scent of sugar, butter, and vanilla wafts in the air around us, as if we've stepped into a bakery.

We follow the smells to the kitchen, where Harper is placing a tray of chocolate chip cookies onto a wire rack to cool. The kids clap their hands with joy, already feeling the rush of sugar coursing through their veins even before they take a bite.

On the counter, an array of cupcakes in pastel hues stretch across the surface like a bed of flowers. The brown color of the countertop creates an illusion of soil beneath the sugary blooms. They look too good to eat, but my sweet tooth is already aching for a taste.

The girls throw themselves into their mother's arms, with Leah holding on a little bit longer while Ella approaches the counter and grabs a blue cupcake. Before she can take a bite, her mother cries out, reaching for it.

"Wait honey, those are for the fundraiser. I made some chocolate chip cookies for you." Harper points to the tray of cookies, and Ella's face falls in disappointment.

Before Harper can say anything more, she storms out of the kitchen, her tiny feet pounding on the hardwood floor as she runs up the stairs to her room. Leah continues to cling to her mother, not letting go as Harper shuffles around the kitchen. Harper looks at me over the little girl's head.

"You know what, Christa, feel free to call it a day. I won't be needing you again today."

My face falls when she speaks. She's barely needed me at all today. In the morning. She got the kids ready herself and took them to school, asking me to spend my spare time with Heather.

"Go on and enjoy the evening with your baby." She straightens up and glances at me for a brief second before putting the tray on the counter. "Troy has a late shift at the hospital again today, so I'll make it another girls' evening." She smiles at Leah. "I ordered in some pizza for us."

In that moment, Ella comes bouncing back into the room, all smiles again. "We're eating pizza for dinner?"

I'm not surprised that she's so excited. Harper insists on them only eating healthy foods and the occasional treat, so pizza must be a rare occurrence in their household.

"What time is Troy coming home?" I ask and Harper seems to visibly stiffen.

"I'm not sure when my husband will be home. I expect it to be late." She picks up a rag and wipes her perfectly clean hands. "A tourist bus was involved in an accident earlier today and the hospital needs all hands on deck, so he'll be putting in a lot of hours." She pauses and gives me a tight smile. "But please go ahead and have yourself a good evening."

My heart shrinks at hearing that Brett is working late, because I really need to talk to him.

"Sure." I smile back. "I wish you and the girls a good evening as well."

As soon as Heather and I enter the cottage, I scan the entire space for signs of Wyatt before locking all the doors and windows, as if that would keep him away. For all I know, he's outside, watching the house.

I clean up, feed Heather, and lie down next to her on the bed. But I'm distracted and I hate not being present for my daughter because Wyatt has gotten into my head. I feel uncomfortable, uneasy, as though something is about to happen.

With Wyatt in the picture, anything is possible and it's exhausting being on my toes the entire time, like waiting for a bomb to explode and not knowing where it is or when it will go off.

Heather fell asleep almost as soon as I put her on the bed, so I pick her up and place her inside her cot, where she turns her head away and continues to snore softly. The sound is sweet, soothing, but not enough to quell my uneasiness.

Back on my bed, I pick up the phone and call Emily.

"Did you get a chance to talk to him?" she asks as soon as she picks up.

"No." I massage the tension from the back of my neck. "I wanted to do it today, but he's apparently working a late shift at the hospital."

"That's too bad. Did you find out anything else that confirms he's Brett Lawson?"

"I don't need to. I know it's him." I pause, wondering how to tell her about what happened. "I saw Wyatt today."

"Holy crap! Where? What—oh my God, are you okay?"

"Not really," I admit. "I was with the kids at the playground and he showed up out of nowhere. It was him who sent me that note."

Emily is silent on the other end, allowing me to catch my breath.

"What did he want?" she finally asks. Her tense tone reveals her anxiety for my safety. Ever since the incident in Austria, she has been overly protective of me, and I understand why. If destiny had taken the wrong turn, I would not be here today.

"He doesn't want to accept that I'm not his mother. He doesn't care about the DNA results that were run in Austria. He found Brett, thinking he's his father. He wants us to be a family."

"Christa, this boy is dangerous." Emily's voice is urgent. "You need to call the police before he does something stupid."

Fear clutches my throat as I recall Wyatt's menacing warning. "He knows we called the police on him last time, and he told me that if I do that again, something terrible will happen. Without a shred of evidence that he's stalking me, I know exactly what will happen if I contact them—nothing, just like the last time we reported him to the cops." I take a deep breath before continuing. "I need to talk to Brett and leave this place. I'll do that tomorrow morning since he's working late."

"I really think you should leave right away."

"I can't do that, Em. I can't leave without knowing what happened to my child. Only Brett can tell me the truth."

"I understand." Emily sighs. "Just be quick about it, please."

I can feel the fear and anxiety settle into my stomach as I

FOURTEEN

I sit up in bed, my heart racing. When I glance at the clock on the night table, I'm shocked to see that it's six-thirty. The last time I woke up after five was in Austria. Maybe I'm slowly starting to break the spell of waking early.

That would certainly be a good thing, a sign of my growth, that sixteen years since I left my hometown my past is losing its hold on me. But I know that until I uncover the truth of what happened to my son, I will always be bound by the chains of my past.

I swing my legs out of bed and go to the cot to get Heather, but she's not inside. It's empty. My daughter is gone.

The cot without her inside is like a bottomless pit in the center of my room. The cream and pink striped fitted sheet is slightly wrinkled, a sign that Heather did sleep inside the cot, and her gray sleep sack lies folded neatly on top.

Panic sets in like a wildfire, engulfing me in its flames, my mind racing with a million possibilities of where my daughter could be.

Gripping onto the frame of the cot, I curl my sweaty fingers tight around the wooden bars, as if letting go would cause me to fall into an abyss.

I pull in deep breaths, forcing myself to calm down, but the fear only intensifies. I start to hyperventilate, my chest heaving as I try to regulate my breathing.

The last time I felt this panicked was when Heather was born and I thought someone had taken her away from me and it turned out to be a false alarm.

Rushing into the bathroom, I barely feel the cool tiles beneath my feet. "Heather," I call out, but there's no answer except for the faint echoes of my own voice.

My heart lodged inside my throat and my head spinning, I dart to the door of my bedroom and yank it open. It's locked and the key is not inside the lock. Someone locked me inside after taking my baby. Screaming for Heather, I slam my hand against the door.

"Open the door, someone," I shout, not caring at this point if Harper or anyone else hears me. "Open the door. Let me out."

At first nobody responds, and then when I call out again, I hear a sound. It's Heather laughing. I bang harder against the door again, screaming to be let out.

"Mom," Wyatt finally speaks on the other side, and he sounds close to the door, "stop making so much noise. You're scaring Heather." On cue, Heather's cries fill the air, and my heart cracks open at the sound of it. She can sense my distress, no doubt. She must also be hungry.

I continue to slam my hands against the door until it shakes in its frame. "Wyatt, open this door. Let me out. I need to feed her."

"Don't worry," he says smugly, his voice even nearer now. "I already fed her. I found some formula."

My stomach churns as I think about my options. I could go to the windows and yell for help, but then Harper would know about Wyatt and everything else. Who knows what he might tell her? But he has my child, which means I'm willing to do anything to make sure she's safe. I'm ready to throw open the window when the door unlocks behind me.

"I wanted you to sleep longer. You were very tired yesterday." Wyatt is standing in the doorway with Heather in his arms, her sobs quieting and her little hand resting on his cheek. It fills me with dread to see them bonding with one another. I wouldn't want my child getting close to someone like him.

"Please, Wyatt, give me my daughter." With my arms raised, I approach him, no longer afraid of anything he could ever do to me. "And let's talk."

"Of course we'll talk," he replies coolly, tightening his grip on Heather. "But first we'll eat breakfast."

Just then, the aroma of cooked eggs and bacon hits me. What is going on here?

"I'm not hungry. In thirty minutes I need to... I have things to do." It's best not to remind him about being a nanny for other kids. That could set him off.

"Thirty minutes is enough for us to eat as a family." He holds on tighter to Heather. "I made us some breakfast. I don't want to eat alone."

Hearing him say we're a family makes me shudder. Left with no other choice, and afraid that he might hurt Heather if I refuse, I follow him to the kitchen. The small table is laden with toast, fried eggs, sausages, and bacon, along with two glasses of orange juice.

"Please sit down." His words are like poison, but I comply, taking a seat across from him.

"Can I hold her while we eat?" I ask, staring at my daughter, wishing I could rip her out of this dangerous monster's arms and run. "Or you can put her in the high chair."

"No, I want to carry her. I want to get to know my sister better."

"She's not... Wyatt, you're not my son."

Ignoring me, he sits down and puts Heather on his lap as he reaches for a slice of toast. But his gaze is fixated on my face, analyzing every move I make. I feel like I'm under a microscope.

He seems so calm, so collected, as if nothing is wrong and this is all normal and not some sick twisted situation. I move my gaze to Heather. She's oblivious to the danger she's in, smiling and kicking her little feet.

I place an omelet on my plate to make it seem like I'm eating, but I can't bring myself to take a bite. My mind is busy trying to come up with a plan to escape with Heather. I have to be careful not to anger Wyatt too much. I already have visions of him dropping my baby onto the floor as a way to hurt me. I can barely force the eggs down my throat; I chew quickly to get rid of the food so that we can start our conversation and he can hand me back my child.

"Is it good?" he asks. "I wasn't sure what you'd like, so I made a little bit of everything." Before I can get a word out, I catch sight of something on the windowsill next to a watering can. The chessboard again.

Wyatt sees what I'm looking at, then he smiles. "You threw it away," he says, eating his food with one arm while holding Heather with the other. "That was not very nice of you. I thought you would like my gift. Maybe we can play a game later?"

"No," I whisper, feeling my stomach clench. "I don't play anymore."

"That's a shame." He pauses and kisses Heather on the cheek. "There's something I don't understand, Christa. Why do you keep saying I'm not your son? But when you were my nanny, you took care of me like I was your child." His expression hardens. "We had so much fun together, didn't we?"

"Yes, until—" Before either of us can say anything more, the doorbell rings.

Wyatt's face contorts into a scowl, and his body tenses up. I feel a tangible aura of rage emanating from him as he holds Heather tighter just as we hear a voice calling from outside. From the kitchen it's faint, but I recognize it to be Harper. But aside from my name I have no idea what else she's saying. It doesn't matter. This is my way out. I hope.

"I'm needed in the main house."

"Go and tell her you're coming, but don't open the door." He puts a finger to his lips. "Be careful."

I want to do what he's telling me, but I don't want to leave Heather alone with him, so I shout as loud as I can, hoping Harper will hear me.

"I'll be right there." My heart is racing, my breath catches in my chest, and a bead of sweat rolls down the side of my face. The tightness in my throat seems to grow with every beat of my pulse. Harper must have heard me because she stops calling me.

Wyatt stands up and leaves the kitchen with me right behind him. In the living room, he opens the curtain a little and peers outside, then quickly draws it shut again. He turns to me and grins.

"She's gone."

"Wyatt, I need to go. I think they're waiting for me to make breakfast. If I don't show up at the house, she will come back." I reach out my arms again. "Please give me my daughter."

He shakes his head. "I have a better idea. I'll stay here and take care of Heather while you go and make that breakfast."

"I can't do that." There's no way I'm going to leave Heather with Wyatt.

"Then how about I play a little game?" he asks, and this time he does not look at me, but he looks at Heather, smiling into her face. "What if I come with you inside the house and tell that woman who you really are? Or even better, I could tell her you killed my parents and I'm here for revenge. Now, that would be something."

"I didn't kill them. You know I didn't." Wyatt's words are

like a punch to my stomach. And the way he's smiling at me, as if he's enjoying my distress, is making me nauseous.

"But your boyfriend did. How do I know you didn't plan the murder together? For all I know, you could be the mastermind behind the whole thing and James went to jail in your place because he found out you were pregnant." He pauses and brings his face closer to Heather's. "James is your daddy," he whispers.

I take a step back, feeling like the air has been knocked out of me. "You're insane. I didn't kill anyone."

Of course, if he tells Harper all those lies, I could convince her that he's lying, but underestimating him could be dangerous. His darkness is so great that if I do not follow his instructions, he could take the life of someone else, or even mine.

"I don't want to leave her," I say even though I know I have to follow his orders. "She needs me."

"Mom, you don't have to worry. I'll take great care of her. I'm good with babies, and she's my little sister. Do you really think I would do anything to hurt her?"

Watching and listening to him, it's so hard to believe that I wanted him to be my son, that I cared so much about him. Even after it was suspected that he could have done the unthinkable, I still gave him the benefit of the doubt. I still cared for him, and now all I feel is fear and hatred.

"Exactly what do you want from me, Wyatt?"

"I want you to accept that you're my mother. Watching you with Heather confirms to me that you will be a great mom to me too. I also want you to talk to my father, tell him who you really are and that you found your son. Tell him you want us to be a family." He points in the direction of the main house. "That's not his real family in there. We are. We deserve to be together."

He's crazy to think that I would go along with his plan. The child standing in front of me is clearly unhinged. It's as if reality itself has twisted in his mind, warped by his obsession with me and his desire to be a part of my life. But I know there's no reasoning with him. He's too far gone.

"I can't do that," I whisper.

"Are you sure about that? Do you want to make me mad, Mommy?" he asks with a menacing tone. "I think you know what will happen if you don't do what I say."

My heart sinks at his words. I know exactly what he means. He's done it before, and could do it again. I have to play along for the sake of my daughter's safety, or at least I'll pretend to.

Trembling, I nod my head slightly. "If you give Heather back to me, I will speak to him and tell him what you said."

Instead of speaking to me, he turns his attention to Heather. "Little sis, if Mommy doesn't do what she promised or calls the police, what could happen?" He brings his ear close to her mouth and nods as he listens. "That's right," he confirms. "Something bad might happen." After that, he hands her back to me and heads to the door.

Holding Heather firmly in my arms, I follow him. When he comes to a halt, my breath catches in my throat. I watch him walk to the living room window again and peer outside for a second before turning back to me, his expression dark.

"I don't trust that woman across the street. I think she's trouble." He looks out again. "She's been watching you. We have to do something about her or she'll ruin our plans."

I want to say something to him, but I have no idea what. My skin tingles with nerves as I take his words in. For Wyatt to know that Madison has been watching me, he must have been stalking me for far longer than I even suspected. He drops onto the couch and flicks on the TV.

"I'll stay in here until she stops watching the cottage."

As much as I hate leaving Wyatt alone in my personal space, there's nothing I can do. With Heather in my arms, I hurry to the room to change out of my pajamas and, when I'm about to leave the cottage, I find Wyatt standing by the front door. My blood runs cold. Has he changed his mind about letting me leave?

With no warning, he wraps his arms around my body and Heather's, and my muscles lock up like steel traps.

"You don't have to be afraid, Mom. I'll never hurt you, Heather, Troy, Harper, or the twins, Leah and Ella." When he lets me go, his words of assurance feel empty to me as alarm bells are going off inside my head.

All I can think, as I make my way to the main house, is that Wyatt knows all their names, and that only serves to heighten my fear.

When I arrive at the main house less than five minutes later, I notice that Brett's car is not in the drive. I stayed up late last night, watching and waiting to make sure I got to him as soon as he got home, but I didn't see him, and I'm not sure if he came home at all. Even when I finally fell asleep, I would have heard the car pull into the driveway.

As I step inside the home, I take a deep breath and attempt to keep my composure despite feeling like my entire body is shaking. Harper and the twins are upstairs as she gets them ready for school.

Before alerting Harper that I'm here, I quickly go to the living room, where the window faces my cottage, and peer out, wondering what Wyatt is doing inside right now. I hate to think he's going through my personal things. I'd wanted to lock my bedroom door, but when he let me out he pocketed the key and refused to hand it back to me.

Feeling heavy, I sit down on the couch, my head in my hands, trying to calm my nerves, but a ball of fear and anxiety sits in my stomach like a lead weight.

Heather squirms in the baby carrier strapped to my chest, her coos and babbling bringing me back to the present. I take a deep breath and stand up, putting on a brave face. I head upstairs to Harper's room and knock on the door. She calls out for me to come in and I step inside, a smile on my face to hide the anxiety inside.

"Christa, are you okay?" I must be so transparent that even Harper can sense my unease.

"Yes, I'm fine. Just a little tired, and I have a headache." I try to brush it off, but I can feel the sweat on my palms and my heart racing faster.

"Are you sure? You look a little pale. Maybe you should sit down." She leads me to the cream leather couch in the room. She's her usual self again, kind and caring, as she sits down next to me. Her hand rests on my shoulder, offering comfort like a warm blanket on a cold winter's night. I take a deep breath, trying to steady myself.

"Christa, you don't look well. You know what? I'll take the girls to school today. Why don't you stay home and rest for a bit? I'm headed to the fundraiser at the club, anyway. I'll drop them off on my way. If you could just tidy up so the house is ready for them to get home later."

I want to reject her offer, not wanting to burden her with my problems, but, right now, I need some time to think and come up with a plan. "Thank you. That's really kind of you. I think I will take you up on that offer. And I'll be able to pick them up."

"Great, that's settled then," she says with a smile before turning to leave the room. "I made a lot of breakfast. Go have some and take a painkiller. Try to take it easy, okay? And if you need anything, give me a call. I'll keep my phone nearby. See you in the evening."

As Harper leaves the room to get the twins, I'm left alone with my thoughts, and I can feel myself starting to unravel, the overwhelming panic taking hold once again. I try to take deep breaths and steady my racing heart.

I sit in silence for a while, watching the sunlight filter through the curtains, and listening to Heather's soft coos. Then I stand up and head downstairs to the kitchen where breakfast is waiting, my mind flooded by what-ifs and worst-case scenarios.

Afraid that Wyatt might still be inside the cottage, I remain in the main house until Harper and the twins have left.

When I finally step out the door, I freeze in my tracks. Wyatt is standing outside Madison's house, staring through the window with both hands pressed against the glass. Her Audi isn't in its usual spot, so she must be out.

I take a step back into the living room, unsure of what to do next. An ominous feeling gnaws at my gut as I recall what he said about Madison being trouble and that we have to do something about her.

What if he's looking for a way to scare her off? I need to call him off before he does anything stupid. Summoning all the courage I can muster, I step back outside, but Wyatt is nowhere to be seen. I scan the street, but there's no sign of him.

A wave of relief washes over me as I realize he's gone, but I can't shake off the feeling of unease completely.

Should I warn Madison about him and his behavior? I can't do that without making her even more suspicious of me. What I need to do is talk to Brett as soon as possible and get as far away from this neighborhood before anyone gets hurt.

When I return to the cottage, I find a folded piece of paper with my name on it lying on the kitchen counter. My heart starts pounding in my chest as I unfold it, reading the words scrawled in Wyatt's handwriting.

I enjoyed spending time together as a family. I'll see you soon, Mom.

FIFTEEN

MADISON

At LaMaya, I return to my sewing room, hoping to escape from thoughts of Christa for just a moment. When I planned this space two years ago, I wanted it to be like an oasis—a place where all the hard work happens but which also has a certain serenity and beauty to it. The soft pastel-pink walls, the pristine white work tables, the carefully selected fabrics and embellishments all come together to create a space where my creativity can thrive. Plants line the windowsills and a small fountain trickles in the corner, the sound of the water soothing my nerves.

As I sit at my sewing desk, the hum of the machine is almost meditative. With nimble fingers, I adjust the fabric and guide it through the needle, watching as the thread weaves its magic across the delicate material. It's easy to get lost in the rhythmic hum of the tool piercing through the fabric.

I came in at dawn because I couldn't wait to continue working on this custom order. This wedding dress, with its delicate lace overlay and intricate beading, is one of my most ambitious projects yet. But as I work, I feel more and more confident that it will be a masterpiece. A high-end customer is getting married and she specifically requested a dress that would make her feel like a queen on her special day. I'm determined to deliver.

There's something satisfying about seeing a customer's vision come to life through my hands. It's almost like I'm creating a work of art.

I have a total of five sewing assistants who work for me in an adjoining room, and they will take care of the matching bridal party dresses. But this wedding gown, it's a personal project. I'm doing it all on my own. I've been working on it for months, carefully selecting the materials and the design. The garment will represent the pinnacle of what LaMaya is all about—a celebration of beauty and style, and the perfect dress for the perfect moment.

My customer is the daughter of a high-ranking politician, and I know that her wedding will be an event to remember. I want her dress to be the centerpiece of the entire affair. Although I don't believe in marriage, I can't help but feel excited about this one.

I let out a curse when suddenly I hear a snap, the needle of the machine splintering. My heart races as I inspect the damage. It's a clean break, and I know I can fix it. In a few quick steps, I disassemble the machine and replace the broken part. In no time, I'm up and running again. But then my phone beeps with a reminder.

Brunch with Harper

That's all it takes for my mood to plummet and thoughts to flood my mind. I lean back and push a hand through my hair, taking a deep breath as I try to shake off the sudden wave of emotion. I don't have time for this.

When Harper and I were still friends, we had brunch every Thursday, and, even if we no longer do, I can't bring myself to delete the weekly notification from my phone. It's like a nagging reminder of what we used to have and what we lost. Today may not be the best day for me to focus on this project as my thoughts keep drifting back to her.

Sage, one of my sewing assistants, enters the sewing room with fabric swatches in hand and frowns at me. I take in her complete look quickly, from head to toe. She's the most fashionable of my employees, always dressed to the nines and with a keen eye for style. She always looks like she's stepped out of a high-end fashion magazine. Today is no exception, as she wears a sleek red dress with stilettos that boast a bold leopard print. Her short black hair is styled perfectly, framing her face in a way that accentuates her sharp features.

"What's the matter? You look like you've seen a ghost." She hands me the swatches.

I force a smile and take them from her. "Nothing, except for a small hiccup with the machine. It's all sorted. What can I do for you?"

"We need to decide the color and texture of the mother-of-the-bride dress fabric now so I can place the order."

I nod, carefully feeling each of the swatches, then quickly check my watch. "Yes, that's no problem, but I have a brunch meeting in thirty minutes at the Lucky Bowl. Can we pick up after that? It won't take more than an hour."

"Of course," Sage says, understanding. "We'll go over the options again when you return."

Before leaving the boutique, I change into a sexy, black cocktail dress that hugs my curves in all the right places. To finish the look, I release my hair from its constraints, letting the waves fall freely around my face. As I rush out the door, I catch myself in the mirror and admire the way the dress accentuates my assets.

Maybe it's a bit over-the-top for a business meeting, but I'm meeting up with Jude Smith, the detective I hired to look into Christa, and I know he likes me. The better I look, the more information I might be able to extract from him.

I chose the Lucky Bowl because it's only a few blocks away from my boutique and I don't want to waste any time. It's an elegant but cozy restaurant, with an oriental theme that brings a sense of calm to my nerves. The restaurant walls are made of a deep red wood, and the lighting from paper lanterns is a gentle yellow that creates a warm, inviting atmosphere. The soft music of bamboo flutes gives the space a peaceful ambience.

When I arrive, Jude is already seated at one of the intricately carved tables, a cup of coffee or tea in front of him. He stands up when he sees me, and I can see the way his eyes track down my body. Taking my hand in his, he plants a kiss on the back of it. "You look gorgeous as always, Madison."

I've always known he has the hots for me, ever since I hired him to investigate my last accountant, who I suspected of stealing from me, and ended up being right. Since then, we've stayed in touch, with me hiring him for random investigations here and there. But I have no interest in him beyond the information he can provide me. He's not at all my type. He's too skinny and on the short side. I prefer my men taller and bulkier. He also appears to be the type of person who is interested in marriage and children, but I'm not looking for something that would commit me to a man long-term.

"Thank you, Jude." I take my seat across from him. "So, what have you found out about Christa Rogers?"

His face droops as he realizes his attempts to flirt with me have failed.

"Why don't we order something to eat first? Have you had any breakfast?"

I never planned on staying long, but since he's giving me his time and doing this job for me as a favor, it's the least I can do. I order a strong, black coffee and a slice of cheesecake and he orders a glass of white wine.

When the waitress is gone, I pretend to be interested in small talk and he tells me about a new motorbike he recently purchased, and how he plans to fly to Asia in two months. He's trying to wow me, but his toys don't impress me much. I have enough toys of my own. But I pretend to be interested until finally he talks about his dog, pulling out his phone to show me a photo of a cute little pug.

"You have a pup?" Now my attention is fully engaged as I lean in close, my arms propped up on the table.

His green eyes brighten with enthusiasm. "I got her from an animal shelter a month ago. Her name's Cupcake."

I can't help but giggle as our food arrives at the same time.

"Cupcake? That's really cute and funny at the same time." I hate myself for sounding so mushy, but dogs do that to me.

His face brightens as he tells me more about Cupcake, and then something shifts inside of me. I don't own any pets, not since my dog, Oscar, passed away three years ago. The hurt still hasn't healed enough for me to think of replacing him. But when it comes to puppies, I'm definitely a softie.

He continues talking about Cupcake until I snap back to reality and collect my thoughts. I clear my throat, embarrassed for getting out of character, getting carried away and almost feeling something for him.

I lean back. "So, did you find out anything about the woman?"

He hesitates, then digs some papers out of his briefcase. "Actually, I did." He studies the page with concentration. "Her maiden name was Wilson. Anna Christa Wilson."

"She was married?" I ask, disappointed.

I kind of thought the woman was lying about being married. Harper mentioned that she had lost her husband and needed help and that's why she was taking her in; I really thought that was a ploy to get into the house.

"Yes, she was married when she was twenty-four in Las Vegas, but, according to my sources, she got divorced a year later."

"Aha." A smile spreads across my face as I lift my cup to my lips, and relief courses through me. If Christa was married at twenty-four, and divorced a year later, there's no way her husband died recently. She did lie after all. And if she lied about that, what else did she lie about?

"Did you find anything else, anything interesting?"

"Yeah..." Jude pauses. "Well, she grew up in Bluefort, right here in Kentucky." He leans back and folds his arms across his chest, as if he has cracked some complicated puzzle. "Does that town ring a bell?"

I reply with a shrug, not really sure what he's getting at. "No, I don't think so."

"Have you ever heard of the Bluefort Cult?"

I lean forward in my chair. "The Bluefort Cult? Actually, yes, I heard about that. It was all over the news a few years ago, but I don't know much really." I lean forward, my head dipped to the side. "What are you saying? Was she a member of that cult?"

"Yes, she was. She was actually married to the cult leader, Jonas Lawson, but the marriage was not legal. I'm guessing she got married again legally after she escaped as a way to distance herself from the cult. But that's not the most interesting thing."

"There's more?" My interest is piqued now. I can feel my heart beating faster, my palms getting sweaty. I place my cup back on the saucer.

He winks at me and this time I actually feel butterflies fluttering in my stomach. "The last people she worked for as a nanny are dead, murdered by her boyfriend."

SIXTEEN

CHRISTA

The air smells of bean and mushroom stew and freshly baked bread. Harper left for her retreat shortly before I took the kids to school in the morning.

On my way back to the house, I did some grocery shopping and then spent the day cooking and baking.

Fortunately, Wyatt hasn't shown up again since yesterday and I could focus on the task at hand without any interruptions. I'm hoping that when he returns, I'll be long gone.

It's now seven o'clock and the twins have had their dinner, baths, and are already tucked in. Heather is splayed out on a travel cot I set up in the kitchen.

I've been waiting anxiously for an hour for Brett to come home, checking my watch every few minutes as the minute hand slowly ticked toward the half-hour mark. Harper told me he would be home around six today and won't be working the night shift.

My chest vibrates with every beat of my heart, my mind racing with possibilities of where he could be. After all the work I've put in planning this day, rehearsing every word I would say to him, nothing can go wrong.

As I pace back and forth across the kitchen floor, I try to shake off the feeling of unease gnawing at me with each passing minute as sweat coats my forehead. I can't let this day go to waste.

Just when I start to think his plans must have changed, I finally hear the distant click of the front door unlocking. My entire body tenses up and, all of a sudden, I wonder if I'm really ready for this conversation. Today's the day I can finally talk to him on his own, and we can reveal all the secrets we're both hiding from the other.

When he shuffles into the kitchen, his tie loosened and hair mussed from a long day at work, my pulse quickens. The air around us grows heavy with unspoken tension.

"Good evening, Christa. Thanks for waiting. You can call it a night now." He glances over to where Heather is sleeping.

My stomach is clenched tight as I pick up a wooden spoon and turn my back toward the pot warming the stew on the stove. "I don't mind staying a little longer. I thought we could eat together. I didn't want to eat alone. I made bean and mushroom stew with spicy beef dumplings, and homemade bread." I turn around in time to see him loosening his tie even more, a deep frown between his eyebrows.

Bingo.

His face is set like a stone as he stares at the stove. He doesn't have to speak—I know what's going on in his head. He knows he's in trouble.

"Go ahead and sit down." I casually move over to the countertop and slice into the freshly baked loaf of bread that I made earlier, following the same recipe I've known since childhood. He doesn't say anything as he walks toward the kitchen table, glancing over his shoulder. His body language speaks volumes, his shoulders rigid. He looks like someone being taken to the principal's office.

I wait until he's seated before I start serving him the food.

I'm so ready for this confrontation because I rehearsed it over and over inside my head all day. I'm also dressed the part, wearing a plain black dress that's very similar to the ones I wore in my childhood. My hair is pulled back in a ponytail and tied with a black silk ribbon, the way I was made to wear it every day. As soon as the food is in front of him, he looks down at it, then back up at me.

"What is this?" His skin is slowly turning red, and I can sense the anger building up inside of him.

"Like I said, it's a bean and mushroom stew with spicy beef dumplings," I reply calmly, taking a seat across from him. "I wanted to introduce you to my childhood meal. We used to eat it every Sunday for dinner. Go on, taste it. You might like it."

"I'm..." He wipes his forehead with the back of his hand, but I can see the beads of sweat forming on his skin almost immediately. "I'm... I'm not hungry."

He pushes back his chair and gets to his feet. I manage a small smile as I watch him stumble to the door.

"That's a shame," I say before he walks out. "I thought we could catch up a little, to talk about the old times." He stops walking and silence falls between us like a thick fog.

For a moment, we simply stare at each other. The only sound is that of Heather snoring softly inside the cot and my heavy and labored breathing. My heart is beating so hard I'm terrified he can hear it.

Finally, he speaks, his voice barely above a whisper.

"I don't know what you mean." His eyes never leave mine and I can see the fear, anger, and confusion warring within them.

"Come on, Brett, don't pretend you don't know who I am and what I'm talking about." I pick up a spoon and dip it into the stew. I bring my spoon to my lips and as soon as the food touches my tongue, all the memories come flooding back, most of them painful. I haven't made or eaten this stew since the day

I left Bluefort. And right now I almost feel like spitting it all out again.

It has been an emotionally exhausting day, surrounded by smells from my past. It's amazing how a flavor or scent can trigger distant memories, making you relive either joy or pain. In my case, it's an unwelcomed place that I never wish to revisit, not even in my thoughts. But I wanted Brett to have a real taste of it.

I force myself to swallow the stew and put down the spoon. "Haven't you even wondered, even for a moment who I am? I mean, you didn't even feel a certain energy about me? Brett—"

"Stop!" He stumbles back to the table and drops into the chair with a loud thud. His body is visibly trembling. "I don't know who you are."

I break off a piece of bread from the loaf, and I'm about to bring it to my mouth again, when I change my mind and put it down. My stomach will not be able to handle the food anymore.

"Come on, Brett, it's me. Don't you recognize me?" I lean in closer, trying to make eye contact with him. "I go by my second name, Christa. I don't have the same surname as back then because I was briefly married once." I bring a hand to my hair and tuck a strand behind my ear. "I know I look different with shorter hair, but, after all these years, I would think that you would know it's me. We were close back then, Brett."

He glares at me, rage and hostility radiating from him. "Don't call me that name," he spits out. He nervously glances toward the door, as if the past is going to come barging in and ruin everything he's worked so hard for.

Most people he knows now would never imagine where he came from. His clothing may be brightly colored now, but back then he wore all black like we all did, and his hair was always kept close to his scalp in a careful buzz cut.

This person he's showing the world is different from the person I thought he would one day become. I'm shocked he made it this far in life, creating something so innocent and pure away from our dark past.

I thought he would turn out to be like his father and all the men in our hometown who never left and never wanted to change. Though I believed he would never break away from his roots, here he is, a successful and confident version of himself. Despite this, however, he still carries remnants of his childhood, evidenced by his choice to take a much younger wife, following in the footsteps of his father, forefathers, and countless other hometown men.

Unbuttoning his shirt, Brett starts rubbing at his neck vigorously and I see it, the last missing piece, the birthmark shaped like a crescent moon above his collarbone.

"That life... that—"

"Is behind you," I cut him off. "I don't blame you for wanting to leave it all behind. I wish I could forget it too, but it's hard to run away when a piece of me is still in the past. I'm sure you feel the same way, which is why you keep going to visit Drew in prison." He opens his mouth to protest, but I hold up a hand and continue. "I heard you the other day. Speaking to him on the phone."

"What?" His face pales and he grabs onto the edge of the table. "What do you want?"

"No need to look so scared. I'm not here to ruin your life. I only have one question."

"What question?" he demands. "What are you doing here?"

As much as it hurts me for him to talk to me like I'm just any other person, like we don't share all that history, I get him. I truly get why he wants to forget me and everything else that reminds him of our hometown.

"I want to know where our son is. Tell me where I can find him, then I'll be out of your life and you never have to see me again, I promise."

SEVENTEEN

The way Brett is looking at me, it's hard to believe that we were once very much in love, that he had once promised to take care of me, to protect me, to help me escape. That hot day we connected in the barn on the farm we grew up on, while working side by side, and the many times after that when we secretly met up at the river to be together, now seem like a distant memory.

It's even harder to believe that we have a child together. How could he just go on, forget about our baby? How can any parent do that?

He must have brainwashed himself enough to pretend the past doesn't exist, and made himself believe he's someone else.

When I first arrived here and saw him, I had hoped that one of his children would be our son, but I was devastated to only find the twins.

"I'm not the person you think I am," he croaks, and I shake my head, agony shooting through my heart as Heather starts to whimper in the cot, as though she feels my pain.

I lift my baby from the cot and hold her to me, wishing I

could protect her from the world I could not protect her brother from.

Many nights I laid in bed, unable to sleep as I thought of where my child could be, whether he was adopted, with a foster family, or in some worse place.

"You *are* the person I think you are, Brett."

"I said stop calling me that." His voice is hard, the muscles in his jaw quivering with anger. "And please, leave my house." He points to the door. "I need you to go and pack your bags and get out."

"Stop pretending you're not him. Your name may be different, but deep down, you will always be Brett Lawson, and I will always be Anna Christa Wilson. No matter how fast we run, we will always be connected to that life, that tainted past."

I did everything to leave my past behind. When I was twenty-four, Emily took me to Vegas for my birthday with a few of her friends, and we joked that maybe I should get married in one of the chapels. I laughed it off, but something in me wanted it. I wanted a fresh start, a new identity. Before the night was over, one of Emily's friends, a guy named Alex, offered to marry me. He said he had always wanted to do something crazy and spontaneous and that it would be a good story to tell.

It was impulsive and we were not in love, but somehow it felt right. So we did it. I became Anna Christa Rogers. Even though we never shared anything more than the kiss we exchanged during the short ceremony, we stayed married until he found someone he truly loved and wanted to be with. It didn't matter to me. I got to keep the name.

But the truth is, no matter how much I tried to leave my past behind, it haunted me like a ghost that just wouldn't go away.

"Brett, I'm begging you to please tell me where my son is and I'll be gone. I'm not here to mess up your life. Have you ever thought of him? Have you searched for him, wondered where he could be?"

"I said you need to go." He stands up again. For a moment he looks as if he's about to slam his fist into the table, but I guess he's afraid to lose complete control.

"I will, I promise. But tell me first what I need to hear. And if you don't tell me, it'll be so easy for me to go out there and tell everyone who you really are." I pause to swallow the lump in my throat. "I wonder what they would think of you when they realize that you are the son of a child molester. Who would want that kind of doctor treating their children?"

I never thought it would come to this, that I would have to resort to threats in order for him to tell me what I want to hear. But, of course, I won't do that to him. Even though we are no longer romantically involved, he will always be my first love.

The threat doesn't go down easy. His jaw tightens as he takes in my words, his fists clenching and unclenching at his sides. I can tell that I've hit a nerve, and I'm not ashamed to admit that I'm using every weapon I have to get what I want.

"Brett, why are you doing this? Did everything we shared in the past not mean anything to you? Don't you remember our time in the barn, our place by the river, the happy box? I loved you, Brett, and you loved me. And now I need your help."

The happy box was a box of things he kept that gave him hope in his bleak circumstances, things he only ever shared with me in a life in which both our happiness wasn't a priority.

Perhaps also visualizing the box of treasures, he blows out a breath before he speaks. Then he glances out the window as if looking to see if someone is watching us. "I'm sorry, but I need you to go now."

Without warning, he closes the distance between us, wraps a strong hand around my arm and guides me out of the kitchen. He refuses to face the truth. It's easier and less painful for him to erase it and move on as though nothing has happened.

"Let go of me, Brett." I try to shake him off. "Don't make me tell—I know about Drew, remember... that you visit him in prison, and I have a feeling that Harper knows nothing about it. I could—"

"Don't you dare threaten me," he growls, but his grip loosens just a bit before tightening again. "If you don't leave by morning, I'll call the police." When Heather and I are standing on the doorstep, he shuts the door.

I shiver as I stare at the door, shocked at what I saw in his eyes the moment before he locked me out. I saw his father, the man with a temper that had the power to hurt and destroy. It hits me that maybe I was wrong, maybe what we felt for each other back then wasn't love.

I was desperate at the time and so vulnerable. I needed someone to rescue me. Perhaps we were both looking for some form of comfort. If you loved someone, even if it's a long time ago, even if it was for a moment, you cannot toss them out the door like he did to me right now.

I raise my hand and curl it into a fist, ready to slam against the door, but I remember Heather, who's now pressing her face into my neck, crying softly.

I drop my hand again.

I don't think I'll get anything out of Brett tonight. Maybe I should let him be for the night, let him think about what just happened here. Let the threat about Drew sink in and go to him again tomorrow. Sooner or later he will have to give me answers, because I'm not leaving until I have them. Once he sleeps on it, perhaps he'll think more clearly.

Even though his own threats felt empty, fear follows me as I walk back to the cottage, holding my baby close to me, looking around.

Surely, he will be too terrified of me revealing to everyone who I am and what I'm doing here. And, most importantly, who he is. The sins of his father and forefathers before him would burn his career to the ground for sure and possibly ruin his marriage. He could end up being shunned by the people he has come to call friends.

As soon as I let myself into the cottage and lock the door, even though I'm not even sure that a key and lock would keep me safe, I go over to the bedroom and sit down on the edge of the bed to breastfeed Heather.

As my baby holds on to the collar of my dress and sucks hungrily, I weep for the man I used to know, the man I used to trust, the man who has built up a wall to keep me out. I rock back and forth, tears trickling down my cheeks and landing on Heather's head and face. Occasionally, she pauses her feeding to scan my face with curiosity before she returns to her meal.

I don't know what I will do if tomorrow Brett still refuses to tell me what I need to know. I'm so terribly sad, not only that he's denying knowing me, but that he's denying knowing our child. That one hurts the most. How can he ever look at his twins and not think about the other child he turned his back on?

As for me, I can't let go of my son. I can't forget him. I cannot forget how he had felt as he grew in my belly. I hope that, tomorrow, Brett's heart will soften and he will admit even for a moment who he really is, long enough to help me find my child.

I meant it when I told him he would never have to see me again after I know where my son is. The last thing I want is to hurt Harper after she has been so kind to me, or to hurt those twins.

When I arrived here, revenge was also a part of my plan. I wanted to destroy Brett because, when everyone shunned me and called me crazy, he did not stand up for me. He did not protect me. He did nothing as I was taken away from my baby, to be locked away because they insisted I was a danger to my own child.

That night is still fresh on my mind like it was yesterday. It was winter, the farm was covered in snow, and the cold air stung my lungs as I ran with my one-week-old baby, who was bundled up in a warm blanket. The smells of manure and dead grass filled my nostrils.

In order to keep my baby safe, I had to leave everything behind, to get away from my toxic life, a life I did not want my child to be a part of.

The day before, when no one was watching, I had sneaked a letter to Brett, trying to convince him that we needed to leave together and start a new life far away. I wanted to wait on Emily to help me, but things were not moving fast enough for me. So I decided to take matters into my own hands.

I asked him to meet me inside the barn where we used to secretly meet, two days later when everyone was sleeping. I had found a hole in the fence that we could escape through and walk the short distance to a dirt road that would lead us to freedom.

But when I arrived at the barn, instead of finding just Brett, there were three other men, one of them my husband, Brett's father. He was a terrifying man with the body of a bear and a temper to match.

When his gaze met mine, I knew I had made a grave mistake.

Brett stood next to him twisting the letter I'd written him between his fingers. My heart pounded in my chest as I realized what was happening. He had betrayed me and our child.

Driven by rage, my husband and the other men said I was crazy and dangerous, that I needed to be locked up for my own good. Brett just stood there, watching as they tore my baby from my arms and dragged me away, never once coming to my defense.

Kicking and screaming for my child, I was taken to a

minivan behind the barn and soon I found myself locked inside a sterile room that smelled heavily of bleach, with nothing but silence and the sound of my own thoughts to keep me company.

Even after what he did to me, every night in the mental health hospital I prayed he would come for me and bring our child, that we would run away together.

He had turned his back on me like everyone else. But, right now, I do understand that he was as brainwashed as all of us were and he had to do what he needed to in order to survive.

After all, he was severely punished for what we did. When his father found out about us, he beat him so severely with a horse's whip that he was left with scars all over his back.

When I was discharged from the hospital and returned to the farm, I found him overworked and starved even more than before. Not once did he speak to me, not even when I begged him to tell me what happened to our child while I was gone. He remained silent and kept a distance until Emily helped me escape a week later.

I am glad that he managed to escape and worked hard to reinvent himself, and I will leave him to continue his life the way he wants it to be, but only after I get what I want.

As soon as Heather finishes, I get her ready for bed and go around the cottage, making sure all doors and windows are locked. Since Wyatt has managed to enter before, even with everything being locked, I place a chair by the front and back doors that would alert me if he tries to come in.

The last thing I do to make sure we're safe is check underneath my mattress, making sure my gun is in its usual place. I know it's not the safest weapon to have around my baby, but I can't help but feel a sense of comfort and security knowing I have it close by, especially with Wyatt lurking around. But it's not there.

My heart races as I search through the room, but it's

nowhere to be found. Panic sets in. There's only one explanation. Wyatt must have taken it while he was inside the cottage alone.

EIGHTEEN

MADISON

I lean against the wall and snatch a breath, unable to believe what I heard.

With my secret key, I had let myself into Harper and Troy's house earlier, wanting to confront Christa after everything Jude told me about her and her past. I had not expected Troy to show up as I thought he would be working late again. But as soon as he walked into the house and they started talking, I could not leave my hiding place in the dining room. My curiosity got the best of me and I wanted to hear what they talked about when Harper was not there.

I certainly did not expect that.

After Troy asked Christa to leave, I'm still here, hiding behind the curtain, replaying the conversation I heard, shocked at the secrets that were revealed. I cannot believe my good luck. I stopped being a fan of Troy a long time ago, when he told Harper all those lies about me being the one who came on to him and not the other way around. I promised myself then that, one day, I would find a way to push him out of Harper's life.

Now I think I finally have the leverage I need. This could

be my chance to get rid of him, so it can be just be me, Harper, and the twins.

Of course, she will be hurt, and there's no doubt that she will grieve the end of this marriage. But after she finds out that her husband is a liar, she would know it's for the best. I love her enough to protect her from this man.

I was spying on Christa, hoping to find out more of *her* secrets, but this is so much better, so much juicier.

Even though I now have all this knowledge, and am ready to confront Troy or whatever his name is, I can't seem to move because my knees feel weak while my head is spinning. Maybe I should sneak out and tell everything to Harper instead, when she arrives back from her retreat on Monday. Maybe that's the best thing to do right now.

It would be more explosive if she confronts her husband with this new information. Also, if I tell Troy what I know, he would have time to prepare more lies to feed Harper. Allowing him to be caught off guard would be the better option.

I push away from the wall, ready to make my escape soon. But Troy is still in the kitchen, pacing from the sound of it.

Since the kitchen and dining room are pretty much attached, if I walk out, he will definitely see me. Then I'd have to explain how I got into the house.

I stay put for a while, going through what I know so far. Jude had told me that Christa grew up in a cult. As soon as I got home after speaking to him, I immediately went online to find out more. It was a messed up one, with older men marrying young girls, who were forced to dress in black and follow strict rules. If what I heard now is true, and Troy and Christa grew up together, it makes sense that he married a woman fifteen years younger than he is.

He married Harper when she was eighteen, as soon as she was legally an adult, so he didn't get into trouble. But in my opinion eighteen is still too young to get married, especially when the man one is marrying is much older. Knowing that there's so much history attached to Troy changes everything.

There's no way in hell someone like Harper would want to stay married to a man who grew up in a cult—his morals, his values, they don't align with hers.

I know for a fact that as soon as she finds out the truth, as soon as I tell her, she's going to let him go, to push him out of her and her children's lives forever. And I will be there to pick up the pieces.

She's my sister and I will do everything I can to protect her and those children.

But now I need to get out of this house.

I strain my ears to listen harder, then, finally, I hear nothing. Quietly I emerge from behind the damask curtain. Pulling in a breath, I take a step, then another, as I move forward, to exit the dining room, hoping Troy has left the kitchen. But as soon as I walk out, there he is, his gaze directed straight at me, sitting in a chair at the kitchen table that's facing the dining room door.

"What the hell!" He shoots out of his chair, jumping to his feet. "What... What are you doing here?"

"I was paying you a little visit." I plant myself in front of him, suddenly bold after seeing the shock on his face.

"How did you get into my house?" His eyes are red like he had been crying.

"After what I heard, Troy, I think that's a very unimportant piece of information, wouldn't you say?" What I have on him is so much bigger than me having a key to their house.

He shoots out at hand and grabs my wrist, tugging me toward him. "What did you hear?" His voice is a low, dangerous growl that chills me.

"Everything," I whisper, moving even closer, playing with him, angering him. "I heard every single thing the nanny said to you. I know that you grew up in a child-molesting cult and you changed your name to distance yourself from your past. Isn't that so, Doctor Brett Lawson?"

His fingers tighten around my wrist and, for a moment, I'm almost terrified he's going to snap it into two. I try to yank it away, but his grip is too tight.

"It's not true." His voice is cracked around the edges. "She... I don't know what she was talking about. You know me, Madison. You know I can't be the person she was talking about."

"All I know is that you are the man who once upon a time took advantage of me when I was drunk. I betrayed my best friend, and you made it look like it was all me. Now it's my turn to reveal to Harper who you really are."

Sooner or later I'm going to prove to Harper who deserves to be in her life. And it's certainly not that nanny or Troy. One day it will be just the two of us... and the twins that I love as my own.

As I watch Troy's expression, I vividly remember last Christmas when he and Harper hosted a Christmas party, and I had a little too much to drink. Halfway through the festivities, Troy found me passed out in their guest room and insisted on escorting me back to my place. When we got there, he guided me to the couch, and, the next thing I knew, his lips were on mine, and his hands were slipping under my blouse.

I can still remember the smell of him, the weight of his body on mine, and my inability to move. Still, to this day, I have no idea why.

"Troy?" someone called from the doorway.

Troy had left the door open, and Harper was standing there. I remember feeling embarrassed and ashamed as she looked at us with disgust. Troy jumped off of me, trying to explain how it was a mistake and how he didn't mean for it to happen. I can still recall the shock and betrayal etched on Harper's face.

Her skin was pale and her hands were trembling. Instead of

hearing us out, she simply turned around and left. The next morning, she showed up at my door, demanding an explanation. I tried to tell her the truth, but she didn't want to hear it.

"You were my friend," she said, her voice shaking with emotion. "How could you do this to me?"

"I didn't, I swear. I was drunk and Troy brought me home. He's the one who kissed me. I didn't—"

Harper interrupted me with a wave of her hand. "I was a fool, Madison. Many people in this town warned me about you —they suspect you've had affairs with several husbands on this street. I didn't listen because I trusted you." Mascara ran down her cheeks, leaving black stains on her pale skin. Her words cut through me like a sharp knife. "Now, I see who you really are. Stay away from me, my children, and my husband. We're no longer friends."

She was wrong about that. I have never stopped being her friend, and once I tell her Troy's secret, she will know that my loyalty is with her.

Dragging me out of the memories, Troy pulls me toward him again. As I fight for him to let me go, he holds on tighter and moves his head dangerously close to mine as if he's about to kiss me. To my relief, he instead moves his lips to my ear and hisses, "You wouldn't dare say a word to Harper."

"Watch me," I shoot back, managing to free myself from his grasp. "As soon as Harper comes back, I'm telling her everything. She'll be devastated, but she has to know the truth about the kind of man she married. I'm not keeping this from her."

Before he says or does anything else, I run out of the house and back to mine, where I sit down on the couch for a long time, running everything through my head again, still buzzing with excitement about the new turn of events, but also terrified at the same time.

When the doorbell rings, I almost don't hear it. When it

finally dawns on me that someone is at the door, I get up. It has to be Troy, trying to talk me out of ratting him out.

I consider not opening the door, but as much as I was a little terrified to be in the same room as him, it satisfied me to see the fear and desperation on his face. The panic that he's about to lose everything—his wife, his children, and his reputation.

I think I'll change my plans. I'll give Harper a call while he's here, and if he attempts to do anything to me, I'll call the police. That should be fun.

I put on a smile and open the door, then my smile disappears.

NINETEEN

CHRISTA

I didn't sleep at all last night, thinking about my confrontation with Brett that had left me drained. But also knowing that my gun is missing. Throughout the night, I was afraid of Wyatt showing up with it, waking up to find it aimed at me. But he stayed away.

I watch Heather, who started crying as soon as I turned to my side. It's hard sleeping with her in the same bed because every movement I make, she's aware of it. Also, sleep regression is a real thing and she relies on me to soothe her back to sleep. But since the day Wyatt showed up and took her, I cannot bear for her to be far away from me. Aside from the usual sounds of the night, I didn't hear anything.

Even if Wyatt didn't show up last night, I still feel the need to stay on my toes, to be careful, to expect anything. He's unpredictable and can appear out of nowhere at any time.

With him out there, especially with a weapon, I cannot afford to let my guard down. He doesn't like to show up when he's expected; he likes to surprise me. I guess he enjoys seeing me squirm with fear. I know he's still in the shadows, waiting and watching.

There's a sadistic side to him. I saw it the day I went to see him at his school. The darkness buried deep inside him can never be quenched. When I saw him again at the playground, I no longer saw a child. I saw an adult in a child's body.

When Heather starts to cry louder, I wrap my arm around her and pull her close, feeding her while thinking of what to do next. The fact is, I'm still here, still in this cottage, even though, theoretically, I was fired last night. I no longer have the right to be on this property. I'm no longer a nanny for the twins.

The twins. My heart goes out to them. I wish I could go to them, to feed them breakfast, and spend time with them for the last time, but I can't do that. I know they will be asking about me today and I wonder what Brett will tell them. He'll probably paint me in a bad light.

I have a feeling he will find someone else to watch them today since it's Saturday and school is closed. After that I'm pretty sure he'll be back to try and bribe me again or physically force me out of his life. He wouldn't want his children to be home to see his angry side, the dark side that reminded me of his father.

The day his father found out that Brett and I were seeing each other, and that I was pregnant, his anger transformed into violence.

I still recall that night like it was yesterday, shivering when I remember every detail, the way he smelled of sweat, cologne, and hard liquor. I remember the burn of his palm on my cheek, the sound of his fist as it connected with the side of Brett's face. That day, he beat up his own son until he was close to death.

The only good thing that came out of what happened back then is my son, and I need to find him. I need to protect him from the world, which I know firsthand is toxic.

After feeding Heather, I hear muffled voices outside. At first, I think it's Brett talking to the twins but, when I put

Heather back inside her cot and look out, I see a police car parked outside the house.

Brett is standing with two police officers, talking to them.

I stumble back as my heart jumps to my throat.

He actually called the cops on me? My heart shatters inside my chest as pain slices through me like a newly sharpened sword. I dared to believe there could still be a tiny piece of the man I once knew and loved. But I was wrong, like I was wrong about so many other things.

It's now clear to me that Brett is as heartless as his father, Jonas Lawson, who may be dead, but still continues to live on inside his son.

What kind of person does that? I'm a mother with a small baby and he's calling the police on me? What does he expect to happen to my child if they take me away? All I want is my son.

It hurts even more that he's willing to risk me losing this child when he knows I already lost one before.

Instead of opening the door before they come knocking, I lift Heather out of the cot again and sit on the bed, waiting for what comes next.

TWENTY

I'm shivering all over as I hold onto my baby, my hand at the back of her head, her little face curled up against my neck. I try not to hold on too tight because I don't want to suffocate her, but I wish I never had to let her go.

Together, we wait for the cops to show up. I have already made up my mind to go ahead and tell them the truth about who I am.

Heather is crying again now as if sensing the tension, the fear, the dread that's coursing through my veins. Of all those emotions, fear is the most suffocating, and inside me it feels like a snake coiling itself around my spine, tightening as it moves higher toward my throat, threatening to choke me.

Even though over a year has gone by since Austria, and everything that happened there, every time I see the police, my mind instantly transports me there, to the hours I spent being interrogated at the station, and that awful feeling of being trapped and helpless comes rushing back to me.

I glance out of the window, still holding onto Heather. I'm just in time to see the cops disappearing into the main house.

This is bad, really bad. I feel it with every fiber of my being.

Exactly what is he telling them about me in there? I could go there right now, to show myself and grab some form of control, because why should I be afraid of the police? I did nothing wrong. I didn't commit any crimes. But something is holding me back from going to expose myself, and I don't know what it is.

I swallow down my fear as I try to calm Heather, who's becoming even more anxious, her mood matching mine. She probably needs changing again and is uncomfortable. I feel as though I'm trapped under water as I take her to the bed and start the process. But my hands are shaking so much that the soiled diaper lands on the carpeted floor, dirty side facing down.

I grit my teeth and pick it up. What will become of me and my children if anything happens to me. With no one to search for him, my son would never be found, and Heather might be taken from me.

So many fears, so many thoughts go through my head. By the time I'm done changing Heather and scrubbing the carpet, my head is spinning and I'm on the verge of throwing up from sheer, undiluted fear. Not knowing what's going on in the other house is making me sick to my stomach.

Luckily, as soon as I've changed Heather, she becomes drowsy, calming down completely. Soon, she's fast asleep in her cot next to me in the living room while I continue to wait for something, anything, to happen. I'm rocking back and forth as I watch the door, as if expecting it to be kicked down.

To stop myself from thinking the worst, I remind myself over and over again that I'm not a criminal. I did come into Harper and Brett's home under false pretenses, but I wouldn't be the first person to lie in order to get a job.

I think back to how I got this job, stalking their old nanny and scaring her off by telling her that the man she knew as Troy was a dangerous criminal and she should stay away from him and his family. I did not go into details, but that was enough for her to distance herself from them, quitting with a simple text.

At first, I felt guilty that I had robbed her of a job she probably needed to survive, but she made her own decision, a decision she could have made even if I had not shown up. And furthermore, as soon as I got this job, I did everything that was expected of me.

I took care of those kids as though they were my own, because I never give anything less than the best for children.

As it stands, there's nothing they can arrest me for.

Finally, I hear them, the thud of their footsteps outside getting louder and louder as they get nearer to my door.

I stiffen and push my hands between my trembling knees, glancing at my baby. She's still sleeping, safe and sound. Still trusting that her mother will protect her.

I tell her every night before she goes to bed that nothing will ever happen to her, that I will always be here.

"Everything is all right," I whisper now to myself as sweat drips down the sides of my face. Then I stand up and open the door before they have a chance to knock.

Now the officers are standing before me on my doorstep, a man with a mustache carrying a large manila envelope in his hand, and a younger woman with poker-straight hair tied up in a bun and glasses perched on her nose. Both of them are in full uniform.

I glance past them and see Brett watching us, his eyes wild even from a distance, and his hair a mess. I don't understand why he looks disheveled. He is, after all, the one who called the cops on me. I wonder whether he regrets what he did, if the guilt is eating him alive right now. It should.

"Good morning, Miss Rogers." The male officer stretches out a hand for me to shake.

He's stout and in his fifties, with a noticeable potbelly pushing against his uniform. His hair has streaks of silver highlighting the darker locks, and his face is marked with the creases of age. "I'm Jason Bane, the Esterford Police Department's sheriff," he introduces himself before glancing at the woman beside him. "This is Officer Carter."

"Good morning, Sheriff." I squeeze his hand and let go quickly before he notices that mine is shaking. I'm not sure whether he feels the sweat on my palm, but I definitely feel like my skin is slick to the touch. "What can I do for you?"

"Do you mind if we come in for a few minutes... for a quick chat?"

"A chat?" I raise an eyebrow, pretending to be confident. "Is something the matter?"

My voice sounds husky and I'm still glancing past them at Brett, who's still rooted to the spot.

I don't know whether I'm imagining it, but I feel like I can see the sweat shining on his brow, and his face is certainly red. What's going on with him?

"Yes," Sheriff Bane says. "We'd like to discuss something that happened last night. Would you mind if we come in?"

"No. Of course not." My voice trembles a little as I step aside.

Soon, we are all sitting on the couch and the sheriff pulls out a notebook.

"The reason we're here is because a woman on this same street died last night."

Shock hits me like a bolt of lightning, and I take in a sharp breath.

He pulls out a batch of photos from his notebook and slides them across the coffee table toward me. My heart lurches as I take in the image of Madison. I cover my mouth with my hand to stifle a sob.

She's lying on the floor, her limbs askew in unnatural angles. Her pale skin is contrasted by the dark crimson stains around her, soaking into a purple scarf that lies in folds beside her.

The sight is gruesome and my stomach churns as I try to hold down the bile that threatens to rise up.

The scarf next to Madison is my favorite pashmina scarf that Emily had gifted me three years ago—the one I wore on my first date with James in Austria.

"Do you know this woman?"

I nod as I reply. "Madison. She is... was a neighbor."

TWENTY-ONE

"Madison Baker was shot last night," Sheriff Bane confirms. A wave of grief and disbelief overwhelms me when I hear the news.

It's strange to feel this strongly about someone I didn't even like. But I'm only human, and it's natural to feel sorrow for anyone whose life has been cut short. It's also a reminder that any of us can suddenly be gone in an instant. The image of her is horrifying.

I gasp as the sheriff stares at me. I know what he's doing. Showing photos of the victim must be a way they try to get a reaction from the people they're questioning.

When I look away, all I can think is that Madison was shot and my gun is missing. Even worse, my scarf was next to her dead body. Everything suddenly clicks into place. Wyatt.

He suggested doing something about Madison. This is what he meant? I should never have underestimated him. I should have done something. I should have warned Madison or gone to the police. But now it's too late, and someone was killed because of me.

I take a deep breath, trying to steady myself and push away the emotions threatening to spill over. "Do you know... who did it?"

"Not yet." The sheriff gathers the photos and puts them away again. "That's why we're here, to ask around and find out who was responsible." His fingers scratch at the gray stubble on his chin as he speaks. "We'd like to ask you a few questions."

"Sure," I reply, although I'm feeling more anxious than I would like to admit. "What do you want to know?"

"When was the last time you saw the victim?" Officer Carter asks, taking out a notepad and pen from her pocket. The sheriff does the same.

I shake my head, staring out the open door again. Brett is still outside, but the twins are with him now. His movements are slow, dragging, as if his body is made of lead.

"I'm not really sure." I stand up to check up on Heather in her cot. "Yesterday, I think."

The sheriff clears his throat. "Did you exchange any words with her?"

"No, I don't think so. We never really knew each other. I'm new here in town and have only recently started working as the nanny for the Wells."

"Ah, yes. Mr. Wells informed us of that." He halts his writing and crosses his legs, his eyes boring into me. "How long have you been working here?"

"A little over two weeks." A small, nervous laugh escapes me. "I don't know many of the neighbors around here. I tend to keep to myself."

A small part of me wonders if the police suspect me. Did they find the gun that killed Madison? Was it mine?

"I see." Sheriff Bane nods, satisfied with my response. He scribbles something down on his notepad. "And did you notice anything strange or out of the ordinary last night?"

"No, nothing comes to mind. Heather, my daughter, and I went to bed early, so I can't really say what happened after that."

I consider whether to tell the cops about my scarf, but as terrified as I am that they might find out the truth either way, I just can't do it. I can't give them reason to suspect me, not now. I can't risk being taken away from my daughter.

"Heather." Officer Carter glances down at Heather, who's now fast asleep, her chest rising and falling gently, her long lashes resting on her cheeks. "That's a lovely name." Her face softens and she allows a smile to tug at her lips.

It's amazing how babies and small kids are able to touch the hearts of even complete strangers. This had been true for me numerous times before—every job I ever took on, no matter how much I hadn't liked the parents, the children always found a way to win me over, even those deemed difficult.

"Thank you." I allow my daughter's presence to soothe my heart and erase away the ugliness for a second.

Unlike Officer Carter, Sheriff Bane manages to peel his gaze from Heather. "So, you're saying that Harper and Troy Wells gave you not only a job, but also a place to stay, and they allowed you to bring your daughter with you on the job?"

I nod, gripping the arm of my chair with one hand as I await his next question, not comfortable about the turn this conversation could take.

He tilts his head back, looking at me with curiosity. "That's unusual. The Wells must be pretty generous."

"Yes, they are." I avoid saying anything more because it's always best to say less.

Some cops have a way of manipulating words to form the meanings that suit them. I can only hope that they can see how lucky I've been—believe I'd never do anything to lose this job.

"Miss Rogers, have you ever had any conversations with

Madison Baker?" His face is serious now and his voice carries an edge.

I take a moment to ponder his question before I finally answer, "Probably." Heather mumbles something in her sleep and, when she falls silent again, I explain. "Just the occasional hello here and there."

It's best not to mention to him that Madison was suspicious of me and had threatened me; I don't want him to think I had a motive for getting rid of her. So, I keep my answers vague in response to his questions.

Hopefully, it'll be enough to convince him that I had nothing to do with what happened to Madison.

They ask me about my relationship with other people from the neighborhood, who I know even less.

After a while, Officer Carter picks up the envelope on the coffee table, pushing a hand inside. His hand comes out clutching a transparent plastic bag, similar to what they normally use to store evidence gathered at crime scenes.

Resting at the bottom is a black cell phone.

"Miss Rogers, this is the victim's phone, and we found a photo of your passport on it." He lowers the bag to the coffee table.

"I don't understand." I stare at the phone like it's a foreign object.

"We also found a number of text messages, Miss Rogers." Officer Carter leans forward, her expression intense. "They were exchanged between the victim and a private investigator. She wanted him to find out more about you. Do you know what she was hoping to discover?"

"I... I don't know." My words stick in my throat as they try to come out. It doesn't surprise me that she was investigating me —she seemed hell-bent on forcing me to leave. But it makes me worry. Will they think I had a motive to harm Madison? "I think

Madison was trying to find a way to keep me and Harper apart. I heard they were close once, but that they'd fallen out. The few times we spoke, Madison seemed obsessed with Harper."

Officer Carter looks at me skeptically. "Do you and Harper Wells have a close relationship that might have made Miss Baker jealous?"

"I wouldn't say close exactly, but we get along quite well. I think she would have been envious of anyone who was spending time with her really."

"Right." She rises up and peers down at me, hands in her pockets.

"Based on what you're saying, is it safe to say that you and Madison Baker weren't exactly on the best of terms, Miss Rogers?"

"I'm not sure," I lie.

"I see." Her tone tells me that she doesn't believe me. "Do you own a gun?"

"Yes." I chew on the inside of my cheek. "Back in New York." I lie without a moment's hesitation. They'll find the records of it anyway. I wouldn't want them to ask to see it.

Officer Carter scribbles something in her notebook, then returns her gaze to me.

"Miss Rogers." Her voice is gentle yet stern. "Do you have someone who can take care of your baby for a couple of hours?"

I stand up from the chair and step back in alarm, feeling like the noose is tightening around me as every action or word tips the scales against me. "No... No, why?"

A pause, and then Officer Carter responds. "We'd like you to come to the station with us for further questioning."

"I don't understand. I didn't do anything wrong," I protest, my heart pounding in my chest.

Officer Carter holds up a hand, cutting me off. "We just want to clear up a few things. It's standard procedure in cases like this. We will also bring in other witnesses for questioning."

That may well be, but none of them have a gun missing, or a scarf found on the crime scene. The more they question me, the higher the chances of me slipping up and saying something that could end up incriminating me.

TWENTY-TWO

"Can I make a call?" I ask when it's clear I will not get out of going with the cops to the station. I had begged them so much to ask me whatever questions they need to inside the cottage, where my child is, but they weren't having it, insisting that either I come in voluntarily or by force.

I can't believe they want me to find someone to take care of Heather, someone I don't know.

Officer Carter nods and I grab my phone from the table next to the couch. I'm about to take the phone with me to the room, for privacy, but the sheriff lays a hand on my arm and shakes his head.

"You can do it here," he says.

Are they really afraid I might jump out the window and run without my child? I didn't want them to listen in on my conversation in case I say something that could get me into trouble. I've done and said enough of that today.

Left with no other choice, I dial Emily's number and press the phone to my ear, listening to it ring five times. She doesn't pick up. But I'm not about to give up. So I call again, but as soon as the voicemail switches on, I end the call.

I need to talk to her, so I try a third time, and this time she answers. As soon as I hear her voice, I break down and my shoulders start to shake with sobs. I can barely speak from the emotional weight crushing my chest.

"Oh my God, Christa, you're crying. What's going on? Are you okay?" I hear the sound of a loud thud as if something has fallen to the floor on her end.

"Something happened," I whisper, turning my back to the cops, focusing my gaze on Heather. I can feel a headache coming, fast and heavy.

"Please tell me what happened. Is it Heather?" Her voice is husky with emotion. She knows this has to be serious for me to call her in distress.

Everything that happened is so strange that I don't even know where to start explaining it all to her. I had not even told her about Madison threatening me the other day. I thought it would go away, that she would lose interest and leave me alone.

I don't even have much time to fill her in on every event that led up to this one. I'm pretty sure that the police will soon tell me to end the call so they can take me away.

"It's one of the neighbors." I keep my voice only loud enough for her to hear.

"I don't understand. What neighbor are you talking about?" In my mind's eye, I imagine her rubbing her ear in confusion.

"The Wells' neighbor," I continue. "She died last night... this morning." I massage my forehead, finding it hard to recall exactly what the cops told me, because everything is a jumble in my mind. "She was murdered."

An audible gasp on the other end, then Emily clears her throat. "Another murder?" she whispers and I look around, making sure the cops are not near enough to hear her speak. I'm still afraid for them to know that I've already been in a situation where a murder was committed.

When I meet Officer Carter's eyes, she signals for me to

hurry, moving her index finger in a circular motion. They cannot wait to interrogate me, to hit me with all the questions, to make me feel like a criminal.

The thought of being considered a criminal makes me want to throw up. I need to pull myself together for Heather's sake.

So I draw in a deep breath and tighten my hand around the phone. "I have to go to the police station for questioning."

There's silence on the other end. I can almost hear Emily's head spinning with questions scrambling all over the place, demanding answers.

"Why? Christa, what did you do?" she asks, her voice laced with worry.

She knows how desperate I was and still am to find my son. She knows that I would go to great lengths to get him back. But does she really think I could commit a murder? Does she think I'm capable of something like that?

I take a deep breath, trying to calm myself down. "I didn't do anything," I say firmly, knowing that this situation will be hard to believe.

"Sweety, I know you didn't. I'm sorry, I shouldn't have said that. But why are the police taking you in for questioning? Why do they think you're involved in what happened to the neighbor?"

"I don't know." I can't talk about the gun and the scarf with the cops around. "They said it's standard procedure. But I have no one to take care of Heather. I'm scared to leave her with strangers." I can barely breathe as I look back at the cops.

"How about Harper?" Emily asks. "Can't she look after Heather for a while? You said she was good with her."

"She's not here. She's away on a retreat... coming back in two days." I pause and lower my voice again. "What if they take my baby away?"

It would have been so much easier if Harper were here because she's the only other person I trust with Heather, but maybe that has changed. Brett could have called her last night and told her everything that happened, perhaps even confessing his true identity in case I tell her the truth.

"You know what? I need you to calm down. I'll get on a plane as soon as I can, okay? You're not alone in this. I'll come and take care of Heather."

I press my fist to my forehead. Even though I'm grateful to her for wanting to drop everything, and even leaving her daughter and husband to be by my side, it will take her at least two to three hours to get here from New York. Right now, each minute feels like an eternity.

Having a friend around would be better than facing this all alone, especially if the police find the murder weapon and it happens to be my gun. I have no idea what's going to happen and I need to make sure Heather is safe.

"Thank you, Em. I really appreciate it."

"Of course, honey. I'll be there as soon as I can. Everything will be okay, you hear me?"

I nod and sniff loudly. "I'll try to believe that." I muster up a smile that I don't feel.

As soon as I hang up, the sheriff approaches me, a softness to his face suddenly. "You don't have to worry about your child. My sister-in-law has a nursery not far from the station. We could drop your daughter there."

I shake my head profusely. I cannot leave my child there, not when I don't know where Wyatt is and if he's watching. It would be easy for him to steal Heather.

"Can I please take her with me to the station?" I ask, my voice breaking. "I promise I'll keep her quiet and out of the way." Surely, she will be safer at the police station than anywhere else. At least there are trained officers there who can protect her if anything happens.

"I'm not sure that's a good idea." The sheriff rubs his chin. "It's not exactly a kid-friendly environment."

"I don't have anyone else who can watch her," I plead. "My friend is trying to get a flight to come here, but it will be at least three hours. I need my daughter near me, please."

"And you're sure nobody else can take care of her?" Officer Carter joins in on the conversation.

I shake my head again. "No, there's no one else. I don't know anyone else in this town."

"How about Mr. Wells? Even if his wife isn't around, he might be willing to take care of your kid along with his."

"No." The word comes shooting out of my mouth before I can even think. I press my lips together, trying to regain my composure. "He's not good with babies," I lie, hoping they won't press me further.

The sheriff exchanges a look with Officer Carter and signals for her to follow him to the kitchen, where they whisper among themselves.

My heart races as I try to listen in on their conversation, but their words are muffled by the closed door. After what feels like an eternity, they return to the living room and the sheriff turns to me.

"You can bring your baby to the station. We have a lovely secretary, Laura. She's a mother herself and is great with kids."

I breathe a sigh of relief. "Thank you so much." Whatever the day holds, at least I know Heather will be safe for now.

TWENTY-THREE

The drive to the station in the squad car is a blur and I pay no attention to my surroundings. I no longer see the things I thought were charming when I first arrived in this town; like the flower gardens that adorn the front yards of the quaint houses, or the playful children chasing each other along the sidewalks.

The cafés the town is so well-known for pass by unnoticed. I don't pay attention to the old-fashioned street lamps and the historic buildings that line the streets. Everything fades into the background as my mind is consumed by my thoughts.

All I can focus on is the pain in my chest, the ache in my heart, and the tears that threaten to spill over any moment now. I try my best to keep them in check, but it's a losing battle.

With Heather in the car seat next to me, I feel so out of control, like my life is spinning out of my grasp. What if everything goes downhill from here? What if I end up being a suspect for Madison's murder? What would happen to my baby girl? Who has my gun? Does the scarf on Madison's body mean that someone's trying to frame me for her murder?

I think back to a time when Brett and I were so close. But people change all the time. As close as we used to be, look at us now. For him to throw me out of his house last night, like I had never meant a thing to him, goes to show that people can change overnight. He could have done this.

As we drive past the Esterford Fortress, I know the station is near. I've driven past it on numerous occasions when I took the twins to school or picked them up. My heartbeat quickens, along with my anxiety. I can barely swallow and I start to hear a buzzing in my ears, like a sound that's coming from inside my head.

The sheriff coughs and I look up to see the police station coming into view. The building is a small brick structure, with a parking lot in front and a few police cars parked in the back. As thoughts swirl around in my head, bile rises up to my throat, but I push it back down. The car comes to an abrupt stop, and the sound of the door opening brings me back to reality.

As I step out with Heather in my arms, the cool air hits my face, and I shiver. The station looms in front of me, dark and ominous. My baby feels like a small beacon of hope in this dark and scary situation.

I hold her close, feeling her warmth against my body, and take one step forward at a time. She squirms in my arms, looking around curiously at the unfamiliar surroundings. I'm all she has, and, hopefully, the officers will see that too.

As I enter the station, I'm hit with the typical smell of police offices—a mixture of cleaning products, coffee, and printer ink. The sound of keyboards clicking almost drowns out the chatter of the officers talking. The air conditioning cools the sweat on my forehead and the sight of the officers at their desks fills me with dread instead of security.

I do my best not to look at anything or anyone, pretending to be anywhere else but here. My head bows over Heather's, her mouth tucked gently into my shoulder as I wrap my arms around her in a protective embrace. She clings to me like a lifeline.

I need her as much as she needs me. Her presence keeps me warm, and I feel as though she is holding my heart in the palm of her hand. But I know this moment won't last forever, and soon the coldness of reality will set in.

"Can I take her from you?" Officer Carter asks softly, breaking me from my thoughts. I nod, handing Heather over reluctantly, feeling a pang of guilt as she cries out for me.

The officer gives me a kind smile. "Don't worry, she'll be in good hands."

After giving her quick instructions on Heather's feeding and napping schedule, in case the interrogation lasts longer than expected, I kiss Heather on the cheek, praying that she will be safe, and that Wyatt won't show up out of nowhere and take her. I have learned not to underestimate him, especially now that I suspect him of being involved in Madison's death.

The officer takes the diaper bag that's filled with milk, diapers, a change of clothes, and Heather's favorite comfort blanket.

"Thank you," I say to Officer Carter as the sheriff leads me away and toward an interrogation room.

As we walk, I keep glancing behind me at my baby until Officer Carter turns a corner and disappears out of sight with Heather in her arms. Now it's time for me to face my worst nightmare.

I take a deep breath and steel myself, knowing that I have to be strong at this moment. I straighten my posture, motivated to answer all of the questions rapidly so I can finish and return to my daughter. The idea of leaving her for too long, for even a moment longer than necessary, especially in a place like this, is unbearable to me.

I have no choice but to quit doing what I came here for. After this interrogation, I'll go back for my things and get a room in a cheap motel until this nightmare is over. It's likely that the police won't permit me to leave town too quickly, regardless.

All I'll go back there for is my car and my belongings. I need to protect not only Heather, but also the twins. Wyatt is a loose cannon, and he's out there with a weapon that could very well have killed someone. I can't bear the possibility of ending up in jail because of what he did.

After a lengthy walk down the hallway, we arrive at the end. As soon as I enter the small room, I'm met with a harsh fluorescent light that flickers every few seconds. The walls are a sickly shade of green and the smell of stale cigarettes lingers in the air.

"Please, have a seat." The sheriff gestures toward a metal chair in front of a desk.

I lower myself into the chair, trying to appear calm and collected despite my racing heart. The coldness of the metal chair presses against the back of my legs, and a wave of nausea washes over me, but I push it down. It will all be okay. I just need to be careful about what I say to the cops. They don't know about my missing gun. They don't know the scarf is mine. I have to make sure it stays that way.

TWENTY-FOUR

I'm left alone in the interrogation room with nothing and no one but my thoughts. The sheriff stepped out ten minutes ago, claiming he would return shortly, leaving me to make myself at home. As if there was any way to make this place feel like home. I almost chuckled at the idea of it, but I held back.

The fluorescent light above me continues to hum in the background, casting an eerie shadow on the walls.

The smell of stale cigarettes has grown stronger, making me feel lightheaded. I can't help but feel like a trapped animal, caged in this mundane room.

The sheriff and his deputies are probably on the other side of the observation window with the one-way glass, scrutinizing my every move. I can sense their intense gaze, trying to penetrate my thoughts, studying every single twitch on my face.

As I sit there, waiting for the sheriff to return, my mind starts to wander. I begin to question everything—my decisions, my actions, my motivations.

My thoughts are driving me crazy, like a thousand bees buzzing in my head. I think that's what they want. Making me wait in here could be their way of getting under my skin, trying to break me, so they can get the information they're looking for.

The longer I sit in the room and wait, the deeper the cold sinks into my skin like tiny needles, the hairs on my arms standing on end. I rub my hands up and down my arms.

It's almost like they have the air conditioning on low to make me uncomfortable, vulnerable, and weak.

I should have put on something warmer, but we left in such a hurry that I didn't even think to ask them to let me change. Luckily, the pajamas I'm wearing—black sweatpants and a matching long arm t-shirt—look enough like regular clothes to not draw too much attention if I step out. The material is just a little thin, so it doesn't offer much warmth.

The temptation to get up and move around the room is strong, to spread the warmth and rid myself of the chill, but I stop myself. I'm afraid the police would see me pacing around due to anxiety, and see it as a sign of guilt. For all I know, my every movement is being recorded.

Rather than getting out of my seat, I press my palms against my legs and take comfort in the warmth emanating from them.

My attention drifts to the clock on the wall, feeling every second tick by as if it were an eternity. I need to stay put until this is over. It's another ten minutes until, suddenly, the door creaks open, and in walks the sheriff, holding a file in his hands. He takes a seat across from me.

I brace myself for another round of questions.

His mustache has a ring of frothed coffee around it, and I can smell the scent on his breath. "How are you feeling?" he asks me and I'm not sure how he expects me to answer that question. He must know how I feel.

"I'm not okay," I say. "I want to see my daughter."

"Your daughter is doing fine. She's a good sleeper, isn't she?"

I nod, and, as I watch him, I wonder if I should tell him I won't say a thing without a lawyer present, but I think that could make me come across as guilty and delay me getting back to Heather.

He stares at me in silence, and I do my best not to fidget while under his heavy gaze.

"Miss Rogers, has there ever been an argument between you and Miss Madison Baker?"

My stomach clenches tight, I shake my head and repeat what I told them at the cottage. "We hardly talked to each other."

"Aside from a hello here or there?" he echoes my exact words back to me. Some police officers don't need any technology to record conversations. They are recording machines all by themselves. "You did mention that Miss Baker was upset with you working for her old friend. Why would you think that?"

I shrug. "It's just a feeling I got. I think she wanted to keep people away from Harper. I guess she was finding it hard to come to terms with the end of their friendship."

"Interesting." He rubs his mustache and his coffee-colored ring disappears. "But it must have been an extreme case of distrust if she felt she needed to hire someone to investigate you."

I'm tempted to let the comment go unanswered, but silence is also an answer, and often it's even better than spoken words. But he says nothing for a while, forcing me to break the silence.

"Maybe she's a particularly curious person by nature," I mumble while looking down at my hands and then back up again.

The sheriff leans back and crosses his arms across his chest. The fabric of his shirt stretches over his muscular arms and I can't help but notice the tattoos peeking out from under his sleeves.

"Miss Rogers, is there anything you're hiding from your

employers, Harper and Troy Wells? Something that Madison Baker could have uncovered?"

"Like what?" I swallow hard and straighten my spine. "No, not that I can think of."

I must look so suspicious right now. I hope he can't detect my anxiety. He's sure to notice. He's trained to pay attention to the slightest details, picking up on words and intriguing pauses.

He gives me a curt nod and opens the file he brought in with him, pulling out a page. "We did get a chance to talk to the detective that Miss Baker hired to investigate you."

"Oh, okay." I stiffen in my seat and my skin prickles with sweat. What could the detective possibly have on me?

The sheriff gazes down at the piece of paper. "He told us that your last job as a nanny was in Ruddel, Austria, and that your then employers are dead—murdered, actually."

My stomach drops as the words hit me like a ton of bricks. I can't breathe, my chest tightening with fear. The fact that deaths occurred in my previous job, even if I was not responsible for them, would certainly make them believe that I had something to do with it and managed to get away with it. I have to be very careful with my answers right now, stick to the truth without arousing suspicion.

I quickly compose myself and put on a convincing poker face. "You're right," I say, confirming what he said. "My previous employers were murdered."

He nods and continues with a blank expression. "We were also told that the person responsible for the double homicides was your boyfriend." He places both hands firmly on the table. "He's currently serving time for those crimes."

"Yes," I respond, though I'm not entirely certain James and I had really been a couple. I wonder how much more the sheriff knows about me and my past, how much the detective found out about me.

"Is he the father of your child?"

I jolt inwardly. Is he even allowed to ask me that? It seems rather personal and not relevant to the investigation. But if I push back, he has the power to make things very difficult for me if he chooses.

I take a few moments before I respond, then finally nod. "Yes, he is." Despite the confidence I insert in my words, I'm starting to panic inside. Taking a deep breath, I continue. "Sheriff, I had nothing to do with what happened to Madison Baker. I'm a mother, and I'd never want to do anything that would keep me away from my daughter. Without her father here, I'm all she has."

When he says nothing to that and continues to stare at me with a critical gaze, I start to feel the weight of the situation bearing down on me. I can sense the tension in the air, and it feels like it's getting harder and harder to breathe.

He's trying to read my mind to discern if I'm telling the truth or not. His posture is rigid and unyielding, his shoulders tense. I can almost feel the power emanating from him. The man in front of me seems to be a seasoned interrogator, and his silence is forcing me to fill it with more information.

My heart races at the thought of being wrongfully convicted. Wrapping my arms around myself, I try to calm my breathing and steady my nerves. I can't afford to panic right now. I need to think clearly and logically. I want to scream out in frustration, to tell him that whatever he's thinking is all wrong. No way will I be brought down for something I didn't do. I lift my chin and meet his stare. I have to get out of here quickly and back to my daughter.

"Sheriff, I'm innocent," I repeat, "but, I think I know who did this."

TWENTY-FIVE

Something in the way the sheriff looks at me makes me very uncomfortable, but I force myself to keep going. No doubt, he's encountered many people who blamed someone else in order to save their own skins. I hope I'll be able to convince him otherwise, so he sees an innocent person in me and not a criminal.

"And who might that be?" he asks skeptically.

I take a deep breath, giving myself a moment to gather my thoughts. I lick my dry bottom lip. I need a glass of water but there's no way I'll ask for a drink. I'm not wasting a second longer in this room.

"The family I used to work for in Austria... they had a son, and he was adopted. He was very troubled and there were speculations that he was involved in another murder that happened in their home years before I arrived."

The sheriff's brows shoot up to his forehead, forming deep horizontal wrinkles. "Another murder in the same family?" he asks incredulously.

"Yes," I nod, relieved that he's listening to me. "The nanny was murdered by the mother; at least that's what the police believed."

"Wait a minute." He presses his fingers to his temples, clearly trying to make sense of all of this. It's certainly a lot to take in and make sense of. "The dead mother of the boy killed the nanny?"

"That's what everyone thinks." I fold my hands in my lap, no longer even cold as adrenaline surges through my veins. Warmth spreads through my body as I continue speaking. "I think they're all wrong."

The sheriff leans forward in his chair, clearly interested in what I have to say. "What makes you believe that?"

I shrug. "At first, I wasn't sure. I thought she did it, but I think it's Wyatt Mayer, their son. He's also been stalking me the last few weeks... or months, I'm not sure."

"You think their son is the true murderer?"

I inhale sharply and part my lips to continue, to tell him everything, as it might be my only way out of this mess. I explain my situation, leaving out any mention of the gun Wyatt might have stolen when he broke into the cottage. I tell the officer when I last saw him, what he was wearing, and the things he said about Madison.

When I'm done, he whistles loudly, the sound bouncing off the walls. "Let me get this straight. This boy has been stalking you because he thinks you're his mother."

I nod, wrapping my right hand tightly around my left wrist in a feeble attempt to feel in control. "I know this sounds crazy, but he *was* stalking me and I think he killed Madison... to protect me. I didn't know she was investigating me, but maybe he did."

The sheriff scribbles some notes in his notebook, his expression remaining serious. Then he looks up again.

"Why would he want to protect you?"

"He became attached to me." I pause. "When he showed up last time, I also saw him lurking around Madison's house."

"And you say Wyatt Mayer is sixteen?"

"Yes, he recently turned sixteen. I live in fear every day that he will do something to me, my baby, or anyone else around me. He's out there and he's capable of anything, and he has an unhealthy obsession with me."

The sheriff rubs his wrinkled forehead. "I'm sorry, I still don't get it. Please repeat it all to me again. Why would he be obsessed with you, Miss Rogers?"

"He has convinced himself that he's my son." I pause as I remember the pain of finding out that Wyatt was not actually my child, followed by the relief of not being the mother of a murderer. "Initially I thought he was as well. That's the reason why I got the job to work for his family in Austria. It was a way for me to get close to him."

"How can you be certain he's not your son?" The sheriff continues to write in his notepad while he waits for my answer.

"After his adoptive parents died..." I clear my throat. "After they were murdered, a DNA test was done, and it turned out that he wasn't my biological son, but he refuses to accept it. But I still cared about him, Sheriff, until I found out what he did to that nanny. That's when I knew that he was dangerous and that I needed to stay away from him. But he still managed to find me and I think he's still here in Esterford."

The sheriff reclines in his chair and laces his fingers together, pushing them into his thick hair. "You really believe that a sixteen-year-old boy is responsible for Madison Baker's death?"

"Yes. And the Austrian nanny. And I also think he's behind the death of the foster mother who took him in after his parents died. Her name was Judy Adams from Cove Haven, Vermont. She died in a fire." I can see on his face that he doesn't believe a word I'm saying. His expression is unreadable, but I can sense the skepticism in his eyes. I lean forward, my voice trembling. "I know how crazy that sounds, I do. But when I saw him last, he mentioned that Madison was trouble and that we should do something about her before she ruins everything for us. And now she's dead. It's too much of a coincidence. I'm scared that he might come after me and my baby next. He's capable of anything, I'm telling you."

A small part of me still thinks Brett could have done this, but despite all the horrible things he did to me, I don't believe he could commit murder, especially since it would put his carefully crafted reputation at risk. Besides, the police wouldn't believe me. What motive would they see for him killing Madison? It wouldn't make sense to them.

Sheriff Bane nods thoughtfully, as if he's coming to a conclusion about the situation. "It sounds like we need to find this Wyatt and bring him in for questioning."

"Thank you. I'll do anything to help." Relief sweeps through me at the sheriff's words, but at the same time it breaks my heart to think of a child, one who's had such a tough life, ending up in the hands of the law.

But if he's capable of killing Madison and anyone else, then he needs to be held accountable. And if he's still out there, he could come after me and my baby next. If I'm lucky enough to find my real son, who knows what he could do to him out of jealousy? For the safety of everyone around me, Wyatt needs to be stopped.

So long as he remains at large, I will remain on edge that someone else would get hurt, that another person will die, someone I probably love or care about, or an innocent person who has nothing to do with what's going on between us. I can't let that happen again.

"Do you have any idea where we could find him?"

I shake my head. "As I mentioned, last time I saw him, I woke up to find him in my cottage. He had somehow broken in during the night, stolen my daughter from her cot, and locked me inside the room."

The sheriff stands up and stares at the glass partition before nodding.

"All right, Miss Rogers, you're free to go to your daughter, but you should stay in town until we get to the bottom of this."

"Okay." I get to my feet only to sit down again because my knees are still weak from the shock of everything that's happened.

He reaches over and takes my elbow to steady me. "Careful now, take it easy."

As I step out of the interrogation room, I spot three officers in a different room, standing in front of a large glass partition overlooking the interrogation room. Through the open door, their eyes meet mine and they quickly look away. They were watching me, listening to my every word. I can only assume that either they think I'm lying, or that fear has started to settle in because of what I said—that the killer they're looking for is still on the loose in their town.

Ignoring them, I hurry to the reception to get Heather. The moment she's handed back to me, I start crying, unable to stop as I hold her to me. After I've calmed down, Officer Carter appears with an offer of a lift.

When we get to the house, Brett and the twins are not home. But as soon as the police car pulls up in front of the house, I see people exiting their houses or peeking out of their windows to catch a glimpse of me, the woman the police have been questioning. A woman who might be responsible for murdering one of them.

On my way to the cottage, I walk with my gaze fixed on the ground.

Within fifteen minutes, I've packed our few belongings, written a letter to Harper, and am back in the car on my way to find a place where Heather and I will hopefully be safe for a while.

TWENTY-SIX

Four hours after checking into the Black Goose Motel, Emily arrives, and as soon as I open the door and see her face, something inside me shifts and I remember the teenage version of her, my first friend. All of a sudden, my past flashes before me, from birth until my escape from the community.

My mother died at the age of nineteen while giving birth to me, and my father followed her six years later after suffering a heart attack. I don't miss either of my parents because I never knew them, not even my father. I did see photos of them, though, and he was at least fifteen to twenty years older than my mom.

No surprise there considering the community they belonged to.

Like all the children in our farming communities, we were raised together and made to think of each other as siblings. But I never felt like I belonged there, always feeling like an outsider.

They liked to say we were one big family, but, to me, we were just workers. From the age of ten, we woke up at five every morning, took cold showers to chase the sleep off, and were expected to help with demanding chores like milking cows, collecting eggs, cleaning the stables, and cleaning up after the animals. It was a hard life, but it was all I knew. At the age of twelve, the work got harder and we worked on the fields for hours on end under the scorching sun or in the freezing cold.

A few hours every day were set aside for us kids to be homeschooled together in a small classroom located in the main farmhouse, owned by Brett's family, the founders of the Lawson Brothers community.

Between the ages of sixteen and eighteen, we were married off to much older men. I was no exception. Two weeks before I turned seventeen, I was forced to marry Jonas Lawson, who was in his late forties. It was only later that I found out that most of the marriages in my community were illegal and were kept hidden from authorities.

Living that life made me miserable and I could never shake off the feeling that there was something more out there than being a farm worker and a baby-making machine, because that's exactly what I was expected to be.

I had heard rumors of a better life outside the community and I was determined to find it. Then Brett and I fell in love, entering into a forbidden affair, and he promised we would escape the community and start a new life together. But there was one big complication. The fact that my husband was not only his father, but also the leader.

Brett and I connected a week after my wedding when we were tasked with cleaning the barn in time for an upcoming harvest festival. It was one of those hot, humid days that made the air stick to your skin like a second layer. My black dress stuck to my back like cling film and my hands were already blistered from the rake I had been using to clear the debris.

There were five of us, and we all worked without saying a word to each other. But then the other three were called to help with preparing lunch in the main house, and it was just Brett and me left in the barn. I continued to work as if he wasn't there because talking while working was something that was not encouraged, a distraction that would prevent us from doing our duties. We were simply robots getting the work done.

"Are your hands okay," he asked, surprising me.

I looked up and saw him staring at my blistered hands. "It's fine," I replied, trying to hide the pain in my voice.

"You can take a break if you like. I'll finish up here."

"No, I'm really fine." But I wasn't, and now that he had noticed that I was in pain, my palms felt like they were on fire.

"Come on, just take a break. I won't tell anyone," he said with a soft smile.

I hesitated for a moment before finally giving in. Brett grabbed a bottle of water and handed it to me.

"Thanks." I took the bottle, sat down on a nearby bale of hay, and watched him work.

He looked so thin and fragile, yet there was a quiet strength about him that shone through as he dragged the rake across the ground, sweat glistening on his forehead. I couldn't help but admire him.

"What are you staring at?" he asked in a teasing tone, catching me off guard.

"Nothing," I muttered, feeling my cheeks flush with embarrassment.

Brett chuckled and didn't say anything more.

"Have a drink as well." I opened the bottle and stretched out my hand.

He stopped, observed me for a bit, then took the water. His Adam's apple bobbed as he swallowed and he wiped his mouth with the back of his hand before handing the bottle back to me.

"I'm sorry," he murmured, studying my face.

"About what?" I took the bottle and took a swig.

He grabbed the rake again and returned to work, but he continued to speak. "You were crying at the wedding."

"Oh." Heat flooded to my cheeks.

He was right. Most girls who were married off were so resigned to their fate that they didn't shed a tear.

"It's just... I always dreamed of marrying for love," I said, my voice barely above a whisper. "And to someone younger than—"

"My dad?" he added.

I dropped my gaze to my hands. "I hate him," I said without thinking and looked up in horror. "Sorry, I mean—"

"It's fine. I hate him too," Brett said, his tone laced with bitterness. "But we're both stuck here, aren't we? Until we can figure out a way to escape."

Escape. It was a word that had been on my mind even more ever since my wedding day. But how could I possibly escape when I was trapped in a life that felt like a prison? As the realization of my situation hit me harder than ever before, I started to cry.

Brett noticed and dropped the rake. Then he walked up to me and wrapped his arms around me, pulling me into a tight embrace.

"It's okay," he whispered, his breath hot against my ear. "I'm here for you."

I felt safe in his arms, safer than I had ever felt before. And for the first time since being forced into a marriage I did not want, I allowed myself to properly grieve my stolen innocence. When I was done, he wiped my tears away with his thumb, but I could see the dampness in his own eyes.

"I know something that can cheer us up," he said. "I'll show you in a bit."

After he had finished cleaning the barn, and before someone came to check up on us, we snuck out and he took me to a spot by the lake. Inside a hidden alcove, he dug a black box from underneath a pile of leaves.

"What is it?" I asked, my curiosity piqued.

"Open it and see." He pushed the box toward me.

I slowly opened it and gasped when I saw what was inside: sweets, chocolates, a stack of playing cards with a rubber band around them, and a chessboard.

"That's my happy box. You better not tell anyone about it."

"But you're not allowed to—"

"I know the rules, but if I'm going to survive in this place, I need something to keep me sane. And that's where this box comes in handy. If you won't tell, I can share it with you."

Anything that brought joy to any of us was against the rules. Sweets were among the many things that were prohibited in our community. So were any kinds of board games because they were seen as a waste of time.

But in that moment, as we sat by the lake and indulged in the forbidden treats, I didn't care about the rules. The chocolate melted in my mouth, creating a warmth that spread throughout my body. Brett and I laughed as he taught me how to play chess.

Since that day, we continued to sneak out to that spot by the lake whenever we could. It became our secret place, where we could forget about the harsh realities of our lives and just be two young people enjoying life's simple pleasures.

Then one day, Brett kissed me, and even though I knew it was wrong and we could both be severely punished, it felt so natural to kiss him back. One kiss followed another, which turned into more. And before I knew it, we were secret lovers, meeting in that alcove by the lake every chance we got.

We were bonded by our love for each other and our shared desire to escape the oppressive rules of our community.

The idea of leaving everything behind terrified me, but the thought of living a life with Brett, a life filled with love, freedom and endless possibilities, gave me hope.

When we found out I was pregnant, we started to secretly plan our escape, making sure we had enough money, clothes, and supplies to survive alone.

My husband had another wife, whom he married after Brett's mother died, but she had been unable to give him more children, so I made myself believe deep down to my core that he was no longer fertile, that the baby was Brett's. I desperately wanted to start a new life with him.

Our plans to escape were shattered when one of the community members found out about us, and Brett was punished severely. I was spared from severe punishment when I revealed that I was pregnant. Still, it was punishment enough to live a life where I was shunned and avoided by the other members of the community because of the sin I had committed.

Then Emily walked into my life. Her family owned several grocery stores in Coldwater, a neighboring town, and one day, she and her older brother were sent to deliver supplies to our community. Emily and I secretly struck up a conversation and a friendship blossomed. She listened intently as I poured out my fears and frustrations, and she promised me that she would come up with a plan to help.

She's the one who told me that what was going on in the farms was illegal and that we had rights that were being taken away from us.

She did her best to come as often as she could and we exchanged secret messages and planned my escape.

I was captivated by her world, and my desire to travel grew. When she showed me pictures of the adventures she had been on with her parents, it made me feel as though I had been part of those adventures too. I was determined more than ever to leave that kind of life behind and start a new one far away with my baby. Brett was forbidden from speaking to me or coming near me again, so I felt like I was on my own.

I was terrified, of course, because a few times there were

girls who attempted to escape and were brought back, beaten and punished severely, or simply disappeared overnight. But Emily told me her parents would help, and, once I was out, they would report the illegal activities to the authorities and would ensure that justice was served.

They kept their promise. As soon as I left the community, seven days after I returned to the farm after being released from the mental health hospital, they notified the authorities. All the farms were raided, people were arrested, innocent children were freed, and the truth about the community was exposed to the world. It was a huge scandal that rocked Kentucky and beyond.

Emily was my friend, my family, and now she's here to support me through another difficult time. She enfolds me in a hug that makes me feel like I've been away on a long trip and have just come back home. I tighten my arms around her, inhaling the same lemon and vanilla-scented perfume she has worn for years.

Finally we let go of each other and enter the motel room. A wide grin splits her face as soon as she sees Heather, who's lying on the carpeted floor, on a small blanket that Emily, her godmother, actually knitted for her.

"Hey there, little one," Emily whispers, getting down on her knees and reaching out to pet the baby's soft hair. Heather giggles and reaches out a small hand, grabbing Emily's long, wavy dark hair that falls over her shoulder.

"She's grown so much," Emily remarks, standing up and taking in the sight of the small motel room. "Are you comfortable in here?"

"Yeah." I give her a tight smile.

The Black Goose Motel is cheap, clean, and it's the best we can afford with the little money I have right now.

Emily nods, and pulls out a small backpack from behind her.

"I brought you some essentials." She unzips the bag and pulls out a change of clothes, diapers, and some snacks.

She hands everything to me and picks Heather up, dancing around with her. She finally puts Heather down again and we sit down on the couch to talk about what's been happening to me.

"Tell me everything." She crosses her legs at the ankles.

Even though she had been laughing with Heather a few minutes ago, her face has now taken on a very serious expression.

I tell her everything that happened since we last spoke, recounting each question the sheriff asked me and my own responses.

Once I'm done, there's a long silence between us as we take in the noise around us. The walls are so thin that you can hear a toilet flushing and footsteps in the hallway.

"You really think it's Wyatt who's behind this?"

"Yes, I do, but of course what matters right now is the evidence the cops may uncover." I let out a frustrated sigh, feeling the weight of the situation crush down on me. "It doesn't look good for me, especially because of the gun."

"What are you talking about? What gun?" She shifts closer to me, her eyebrows furrowed with concern. "Whose gun?"

I hesitate, unsure if I should tell her, since I know how she will react. But I can't find it in me to lie to my best friend.

"I had a gun that I kept under my mattress. I checked on it last night and it's gone."

"Bloody hell, Christa—why on earth do you have a gun? What were you thinking?"

"I was thinking that I wanted to protect myself and my daughter. That day in the hospital, when we found out about the death of Wyatt's foster mother, Heather disappeared from the room and I thought someone had taken her. But it ended up being one of the nurses, who had taken her to the nursery for feeding. But after that, I felt like I needed to be prepared for anything."

Emily pauses for a moment, staring at me with a mix of shock and disapproval. "You can't just go around with a gun, Christa. There are other ways to protect yourself and Heather."

"I know, I know," I say, feeling defensive. "It's just that Wyatt was out there and you know what he's capable of. The point is, now the gun is gone and I have no idea where it could be. I'm just terrified that—"

"That it's the weapon that was used to kill the neighbor?" Emily rubs her forehead with her fingertips, trying to absorb the gravity of the situation. "You need to tell the cops about this. If you say nothing, it will only make you look more suspicious."

I nod reluctantly, knowing that she's right. "I thought of doing that, but there's something else too," I say, my voice barely above a whisper. "The cops showed me the crime scene photos and my scarf was next to the body. The scarf you bought me. That's why I can't tell them about the gun... or that the scarf is mine."

Emily's hand flies up to her mouth. "Oh my God," she whispers. "Christa... how... how did your scarf end up there?"

"I don't know. It could have been Brett wanting to frame me. But it could also be Madison who took it from the cottage." It could also be Wyatt, since I still suspect it's him who took my gun and possibly killed Madison, but as obsessed as he is with me, I don't want to believe he would want to hurt me, not like that.

"You mean when she took a photo of your passport?"

I nod. "I could end up in jail for a crime that I didn't commit. I can't be taken away from my child."

"That won't happen." Emily grips my hand tight. "We can't do anything about the scarf, but we need to find that gun before the cops do. We need to find Wyatt and get him to confess. I also think he's the one who killed that woman. But before we search for him, I'm moving you and Heather out of this motel. You need to stay somewhere more comfortable and secure."

* * *

I'm thankful to Emily for getting us a room at the Maryway, the only five-star hotel in town, but I also can't help but feel guilty because I know how expensive it is.

"Really, I didn't mind staying at the Black Goose," I tell her.

"Hey, don't feel guilty." In the lobby, she takes me by the shoulders. "For two years now, George keeps telling me to spend the money my parents left me. I never found anything worth splurging on, until now. And besides, I think you and Heather will be safer here than in that motel—there's a doorman, proper locks on the doors, and we're a few flights up. Now let's go up to the room. You need to relax."

The suite is luxurious and airy, with a chic modern design of calming hues of gray, blue, and white. The walls are decorated with wooden paneling, which adds a warm atmosphere.

In the background, you can hear the low hum of the air conditioner mingling with the sweet smell of flowers in vases around the room. A gigantic king-size bed stands in the middle of the room highlighted by fluffy pillows in different shades of blue. From our window, we have an amazing view of the town below.

The fortress is visible in the distance, soaring into the sky and casting its regal presence over the entire town. The bathroom is equally impressive, with marble countertops, a large Jacuzzi in the corner, and a walk-in shower that looks like something out of a spa, complete with a rainfall showerhead and multiple jets for a full-body massage.

As I eye the shower, a wave of exhaustion hits me. It's been a long day, and I can feel my muscles protesting against the tension they've been holding since it all started. Without thinking twice, I strip off my clothes and step under the cold spray to scrub all the dirt and grime from my skin and hair. When I step out of the shower, the fragrant scents of lavender body wash and shampoo waft around me. I grab a fluffy white towel and wrap it around my body before entering the spacious bedroom, where Emily and Heather are waiting for me.

Emily points to my phone on the bedside table. "You got several calls while you were in the shower. I didn't check to see who it is."

The first thought that pops into my mind is that it's the police. I haven't told them my new location yet.

"Oh, thanks." My heart in my throat, I pick up the phone and see a series of missed calls from Harper. But rather than feel relieved that it's not the cops calling to tell me they found my gun, my anxiety spikes at the thought of Harper trying to reach me. I haven't spoken to her since she left for her retreat.

"Who is it?" Emily hoists Heather up on her hip, glancing first at my face then at the phone.

"It's Harper." I put the phone down only for it to ring again almost immediately. I take a deep breath and answer it. "Hi, Harper."

"Christa, hey. I just read your letter and I'm kind of lost." Her voice is stuffy, like she has been crying.

"You're back in town?" I ask, giving myself time to think.

She blows her nose loudly on the other end. "Yes, when I heard about Madison, I had to come back early. It's terrible what happened..." She goes silent for a long time, making no sound except for the occasional sniffle.

I feel my heart wrench at the sound of her pain, knowing that I cannot tell her my suspicions about Wyatt until I find him and my gun.

"I cared about Madison, you know," she says finally. "She used to be like a sister to me. Things went wrong between us and we had a falling out, but she didn't deserve to die, no one does. And not like that. I keep wondering who would do such a thing to another human being. What goes on through their head? It's so cruel and senseless. When Troy called to tell me she died, I... I couldn't believe it. I kept thinking it was all a nightmare and that I would wake up any minute, but it never happened. Despite what happened between us, I miss her so much, and it hurts to think we'll never get the chance to make amends."

"Harper, I'm so sorry for your loss. I really hope they will find whoever did this and bring them to justice. And I'm really sorry that I had to quit the job so suddenly."

"Why did you? I thought you liked working for us. We did everything to make sure you're comfortable. The twins really liked you and Heather."

"I know and we really did enjoy staying with you, but, to be honest, I underestimated how much work it would be for me to babysit with a small baby. I thought I could handle it but I can't."

"Oh, I thought your schedule was quite flexible. It's a shame you couldn't manage it." Harper sounds disappointed, and I can't blame her.

"I'm really sorry, Harper. I didn't want to let you down. I should have talked to you instead of leaving a letter." She deserves to know at least part of the reason why I left. She was so kind to me and Heather. "There were other reasons as well. Can we meet in person to talk about it?"

"Sure, but I just arrived at the police station. They asked me to come in for questioning. I'll also be busy most of the day tomorrow. I'll be planning a get-together at the club in honor of Madison. How about I call you tomorrow evening and we can discuss when to meet? I have to go."

"Yeah, sure. Take care. And good luck with the questioning."

I hang up the phone and sink onto my bed, feeling a heavy

weight on my chest. Telling Harper that I lied to her about my motivations to work for her won't be easy. But it needs to be done. She deserves to know who her husband really is.

She's also a mother. Maybe one day she will find it in her heart to forgive me and might even be willing to help me find my son. She might be able to get through to Brett.

TWENTY-SEVEN

I'm jarred from sleep by a loud and insistent banging on the door. At first, I think it's part of my dream, but soon realize the noise is much too real and close by to be imagined.

Groaning, I roll over and squint at the clock—it's only four in the morning. Who would come knocking on someone's door this early?

"What in the world?" Emily whispers, pulling the covers over her head to get back to sleep. She's not a morning person and hates nothing more than getting up before the sun.

We're sharing the same bed with Heather nestled between us. To protect her from our tossing and turning, we've wedged her between our pillows, forming a cozy nest. But it doesn't really matter because knowing she's in bed with us is reason enough for me to not drift into a deep sleep, aware of every breath she takes and every movement she makes.

Right now, Heather is fast asleep, her little fists clenched tightly and her breathing slow and steady. Her mouth is slightly open, making a soft whistling sound, and her innocent face is a picture of serenity. I'm surprised she can still sleep with all the commotion outside.

The banging grows louder and more insistent like the person outside is trying to break down the door. Despite the fact that Emily and I had been talking late into the night, discussing my situation, I feel surprisingly well-rested this morning.

Maybe it's the fact that I'm not alone. Knowing Emily is here with me has brought a sense of security and comfort. She had been an immense help last night, from assisting with some of Heather's night feedings, to changing her diapers, and rocking her back to sleep.

Although she urged me to get some rest, to conserve my energy for the rocky road ahead, I insisted on helping with Heather as well. I wanted to spend as much time as I could with my daughter in case something happens that takes me away from her.

Emily promised me that she's planning to stay for a week in the hopes that things will be resolved by then, and the three of us can return together to New York.

"I won't leave this place without you," she had said with determination.

Even though I haven't yet made my mind up whether I want to return to New York or start over in a new place, I didn't fight her since I have no idea where I want to go anyway, which place would make me feel safe. As long as Wyatt is out there, does it really matter where I go? I have a feeling he will always find me.

The banging continues, reverberating off the walls of our hotel room. I sit up abruptly, ignoring Emily's grumbling, and throw on a robe. Emily throws back the covers and sits up as well, suddenly alert.

We exchange a look of wariness before I head to the door.

I peek through the peephole and see a man with a full, thick beard that almost covers his entire face, and a deep scowl that makes him look intimidating. Another man is standing next to him, but I can only make out the thick outline of his left shoulder. One thing that stands out is the gleaming piece of metal on the visible man's chest.

My heart lodges itself into my throat as I turn to Emily. Her face falls as I mouth the word: "Police."

After talking to Harper yesterday, I did contact the station to let them know where I'm staying, but what are they doing here at this hour? It could be good news, I tell myself, as I shake my hands to rid them of the nervous tremors coursing through my body. Maybe they found Wyatt and came to tell me in person. Or they're here for another reason entirely, one I can't bear thinking about.

Emily has her arms around her body, her expression one of terror. She scrambles over and wraps her arms tightly around me. We stay like that for a little while until we break away from each other.

"Miss Rogers, please open the door."

How do they know I'm standing behind the door? I take a deep breath and slowly unlock the deadbolt, pulling the door open just enough to see the two men on the other side.

"Good morning, officers." I try hard to sound calm and composed. "Is there something I can help you with?"

"May we come in, miss?" The bearded man's voice carries a hint of impatience.

I hesitate for a moment, glancing back at Emily. She shakes her head ever so slightly, and I know that she doesn't want them to come in either. What if they found enough evidence to arrest me?

Whatever the case, I can't deny the police entry. I clear my throat, nod my head, and step aside to let them in.

The cop whose face had been hidden from view steps forward, looking past me into the room. Perhaps in his mid-thirties, he looks at least ten years younger than the other officer, and his face is clean shaven, highlighting his youthfulness.

There's a scar above his right eyebrow that gives him a rugged edge.

The older man clears his throat. "Miss Rogers, I'm Detective Jensen, the lead detective in the Madison Baker investigation, and we would like to ask you a few more questions." He scans the room before settling his attention on me, and I can feel the weight of his stare as it lingers on my face. I can't help but notice the gun hanging low on his hip.

Making himself feel at home, he walks past me and takes a seat on one of the chairs at the table by the window. He motions for me to sit in the chair opposite him, but I don't move. Instead, I stand shakily, watching as he pulls out a notepad and pen. I glance at Emily, whose face is a mask of fear as she stands by the door to the bedroom with Heather in her arms.

Now awake, Heather is sucking on her little fist, making it shine with baby drool. My heart aches as I think about her innocent little life and how it could be affected by whatever is about to happen here.

After the other officer sits down on the couch, I take a deep breath and sit down in the chair across from Detective Jensen, trying to keep a calm expression on my face.

"Detective, I was already questioned yesterday, and I told the sheriff everything I know." My voice comes out more steady than I thought it would.

Detective Jensen looks at me for a few seconds, studying my face. "Miss Rogers, we have reason to believe that you may have left out some important details in your previous statement. We need to ask you a few more questions to get a better understanding of what happened the night Madison Baker died."

To my horror, he pulls out the crime scene photos again, and slides them across the table toward me. My stomach churns again at the sight of Madison's lifeless body, her face now distorted in death. The graphic nature of the photos causes me to feel sick. I take a deep breath, trying to hold myself together.

"You never mentioned that the scarf found next to the victim's body belongs to you."

"I... I didn't realize it was mine," I stammer.

"I see." He raises an eyebrow, his pen poised over the notepad. "Not only that, but we also have reason to believe that you had motive to harm Madison. Is there anything you'd like to tell us?"

"What motive?" I manage to whisper, my mind spinning with confusion and fear. "I didn't have any reason to hurt her." I barely knew Madison; why on earth would I want to harm her?

The detective leans forward, then he pulls out more photos and places them in front of me.

"These are copies of photos sent to the police from an anonymous source."

My mouth drops open as I stare at them, studying them, trying to understand what's happening.

They are photos of me and Madison talking to each other inside Harper and Brett's bedroom the day she caught me snooping around. It's hard to miss the angry expressions on both our faces.

The person who sent them was watching us, or, better yet, watching me. It doesn't take a rocket scientist to know who that is.

"He was planning this all along," I murmur. "He knew from the start that he was going to frame me for murder. He collected the evidence." I run a frustrated hand through my hair. Wyatt had seemed so genuine when he'd said he wanted us to be a family. I know he's troubled and has done terrible things, but I didn't think he'd ever hurt me. But now I'm not so sure.

"It must have been him," I say. "I'm being set up by Wyatt."

"The sixteen-year-old boy you told the sheriff about?" Detective Jensen jots some notes in his notebook, his expression remaining serious. Then he looks up again. "Wyatt Mayer is his name, right?"

"Yes, Detective." I clench my fists under the table, trying to control my anger. "A dangerous sixteen-year-old boy, who confessed to my face that he killed someone. I believe he murdered Madison Baker and is trying to pin the murder on me."

"Why would he do that?"

Doing my best not to explode, I repeat to him everything I already told the sheriff, even though I know he was updated and he's just trying to get me to slip up.

When I'm done, I glance behind me, looking for Emily, but she's no longer there. I can hear my daughter's soft giggles coming from the room. They do nothing to soothe me. I turn back to the detective and ask him a difficult question.

"Do I need a lawyer?"

Detective Jensen leans back in his chair and regards me carefully.

"Miss Rogers, I want to make it clear that we're not charging you with anything right now. We're just trying to get to the bottom of this." He pauses to glance at his colleague then back at me. "But if you feel more comfortable having a lawyer present, that's your right."

I nod slowly, taking a deep breath to calm my racing heart. "I understand. Thank you, Detective."

He nods back and closes his notebook. "We'll be in touch with you soon with more updates. In the meantime, don't leave town. And if you have any more information, don't hesitate to contact us."

As soon as the cops leave the room, Emily returns to the living room without Heather and wraps her arms around me. And just like that, I break. My emotions, which I've been trying to hold in, spill out as I hug her tightly. The fear, the anger, the sadness, all of it comes out in sobs. Emily doesn't say anything, she just holds me as I cry. After a few minutes, I manage to pull myself together.

She hands me a glass of water and sits down next to me. “My uncle Clifford is a lawyer. Should I—”

“No.” I put down the glass without taking a sip. “I think getting a lawyer would make me look guilty. I didn’t do anything wrong, Emily.”

She nods in understanding and squeezes my hand. “But what if they find the gun next?”

“I don’t know.” I sigh. “I don’t understand why Wyatt didn’t just leave it at the crime scene. I guess he wants to torture me bit by bit.” But what he doesn’t know is that I won’t go down without a fight.

TWENTY-EIGHT

In the evening, Emily and I are about to head downstairs for dinner when we open the door to find Brett standing there, a brown leather briefcase in his hand.

"Christa, we need to talk," he announces. Then, without asking for permission to enter, he walks through the door.

"I'll give you a moment." Emily takes Heather from me and heads to the room, closing the door behind them.

"What do you want to talk to me about, Brett, and how did you know where to find me?"

He has settled on the living room couch, looking flustered. His hair is a mess with some of it sticking up in odd angles, and there are bags under his eyes. He looks like he hasn't slept in days. "It's not hard to find someone in a small town. People around here talk." His expression is blank, on the verge of ice-cold. "I heard the police questioned you again."

"Yeah." I fold my arms across my chest and deny myself the urge to say more. If he thinks I'm going to fill him in on the details of my interrogation, he's got another think coming. "Why are you here, Brett?"

I doubt very much that he's here to help me in any way. He

looks down at the briefcase he brought with him. "I'm here to make you a deal." His gaze shifts back up to meet mine.

"Let me guess. You want me to leave town and take your secrets with me?" As long as I'm in this town, I'm definitely a threat to him.

He sighs and then runs a hand through his hair. "Look, this has nothing to do with you as a person. And you were right, we *did* have a connection. But that's in the past. I'm not the person I used to be and you have changed as well."

My head snaps back. I had only meant it as a joke, but, judging from his reaction, I clearly hit the nail of truth on the head. "You can't be serious, Brett. How could you even think that I would consider leaving town? I'm sure the cops told you and everyone else that were questioned about Madison's death that we're not allowed to leave town. If I don't respect that rule, I might end up looking guilty, wouldn't you say? Wait"—I point to the briefcase—"is there money in there? You want to pay me to go away?" I cover my face with both hands then drop them again. "Wow! It was no secret that your dad had cash from treating his followers like servants, but, clearly, he left you more than I imagined, if you're being so awfully generous."

He grabs my hand and squeezes my fingers so hard that pain shoots up my arm, making me wince. "Don't you dare talk about my father that way again, Anna."

It's the first time he has called me by the name I was known by back then. I'm so taken aback that I don't answer right away. Even more shocking is that he's sticking up for his dad, an abuser, the monster we had both longed to escape from. The man who stole my childhood. He saw it all, all the pain around him, and he's defending him.

He lets go of me and pulls away, exhaling loudly. "Listen, I've made something of my life here. I have built a career. I'm making an impact in this community and people respect me for it." He pauses to glance at the door Emily and Heather disappeared through. "I know my father did many terrible things. But he's gone now, and he left me his fortune. I can use it to help you start a new life somewhere else. Away from all of this." Brett's lips are pressed together in a thin line as he stares at me.

I massage the hand he had squeezed, feeling a lump form in my throat. For a split second, I entertain the idea of accepting his offer. A new life away from all of this may be just what me and Heather need. But then, a different kind of anger bubbles up inside me, stopping me in my tracks. "Do you seriously think that giving me money will solve everything, Brett? I only want—"

"Troy," he corrects, his tone edged with steel. "My name is Troy now." He wedges the briefcase between his feet. "You can't do this... just show up and disrupt what I worked so hard for. I'm not part of that life anymore. I'm nothing like my father."

I shift away from him. "Well, you married a woman much younger than you, just like he did. How old was Harper when you got married, eighteen, nineteen? Pretty young, don't you think?"

He reels back, scowling, his lips curled in a sneer. "Don't you dare compare me to him." He spits the words out like an arrow flying from a bow.

His anger is palpable, and I can feel myself wanting to shrink away from him. But I stand my ground.

"You may not be exactly like him, but you're not exactly a saint, either. Are you?"

"This is different." He slams his fist against his forehead as he speaks. "I'm different. Harper and I... are... we fell in love. Don't you see? I have a wife and kids to think about."

"That's great, but what about your other child? The one who might be out there, struggling? Ever think about him?"

"There is no child. I'm really sorry, but the baby died. I

know it's hard for you to accept, but it's time for you to come to terms with it."

"That's not true." I leap up and fling open the windows. My chest tightens as if my lungs are shrinking in size. How could he be so callous, to speak like that about our child, with no emotion whatsoever? It's almost as if he has no feelings at all.

I grasp my neck with one hand while struggling to take a breath. Pushing my head out the window, I gulp in as much air as possible. But no matter how much oxygen I take in, the dizziness and panic only increases. I shut my eyes, and all I see are stars dancing before me.

Brett remains silent, his presence looming behind me. Why is he still lying to me despite the years that have passed? Why doesn't he want to soothe my anguish or lighten up this suffocating darkness? The overwhelming feeling eventually dissipates, though I'm still shaking and sweating. Once I can catch my breath again, I turn to face him, watching as he sits back on the couch. It's incredible that he isn't as affected by this as I am.

"I know what happened." I stumble back to the couch. "They never wanted our child to be born. That's why they took him away. He was too much a reminder of what happened, a stain on the community. They made me believe I was crazy and sent me to that place, so they could take my baby."

Rage coursing through me, I grab his arm and yell. "How could you let this happen? How could you let them take him? I... I thought you loved me." My fists hit his chest as sobs overwhelm me. "I tried so hard to protect our baby from them, and they took him away from me." As much as I want to believe him, I can't shake off this nagging doubt that he's hiding something.

He clasps my wrists firmly. "Anna, it's time to let go of this. It won't help you get your baby back. Stop dwelling on the past. Now is your chance to create a fresh life for yourself and your child. I'm giving you this opportunity. Please, take it."

"You're wrong," I shout, my hand trembling as I point a

finger at him. "As long as I know my child is out there, I will always keep looking back. Real parents don't move on without their children." I grab a cushion, and press it tight to my abdomen as a realization hits me. "Did you do this? Did you kill Madison and try to pin it on me? You did threaten to call the police on me."

I'm still suspecting Wyatt, but I need to cover all bases just in case.

"No, no, Anna. I would never..." Brett stammers. "I'm not a murderer." He leans forward, his volume dropping as if someone might overhear him. "I didn't do it, but I did hear that the police found evidence that points to you being—" He clears his throat. "Your scarf was found on the scene, and there are other things that make you look guilty."

I wrap my hand around my throat again, feeling like I'm suffocating. "It was you who told them it was my scarf?"

"They asked me if I recognized it, and I did. I couldn't lie to the police. You wore it the day you moved into our house." He pauses. "I have no idea how it got to Madison's house, because, for all it's worth, I don't believe you had anything to do with it. But the fact is, the police found evidence that could implicate you in her murder. The cops have a way of making things fit their narrative." He rubs his stubble. "It doesn't help that two murders happened to occur around you. It doesn't look good for you, Anna."

"Two murders?" As his words sink in, blood drains from my face. "How... How do you kn—"

"That your last employers were murdered and you conveniently chose not to mention it to us? It doesn't matter how I know, and, right now, I don't really care what did or didn't happen. What's important is that, of all the people in our neighborhood, you are the person the police will be looking at the closest. If you don't take this deal, there's a possibility you might end up in prison for murder and Heather will grow up without a mother." He blows out a breath. "My advice to you is to get as far away from this town as you can. Accept my offer so you can be with your baby. There's plenty in that briefcase for you to get started again." He lifts the suitcase and sets it down in front of me. "All you have to do is take the money and run before it's too late. Sooner or later, the police will return, and who knows what kind of evidence they'll find next. I'm not only giving you this money, but I have connections. I can help you disappear."

I stare at the suitcase, my mind racing with the gravity of the situation. Then I meet his gaze and shake my head. "You're willing to pay so much for me to go away, so Harper never finds out who you really are? Why don't you just tell her the truth about your identity? She's a wonderful person. She might understand."

"I can't. I can't reveal that I lied to my wife, not revealing my true identity. She's already going through so much right now after losing someone she used to care about. I can't afford to put her through this as well." He rakes his fingers through his hair and then throws his hands in the air before letting them fall back into his lap. "I know you care about Harper and she feels the same way about you. So, if not for me, at least do it for her. Think about what this would do to her."

I can't help wondering if Harper told him that we're planning to meet up. Now that I no longer work for them, he probably suspects I might tell her the truth about him, and he's right. She deserves to know.

"I can't take your offer, Brett. I'm innocent, but, if I leave town now, it'll look like I'm guilty."

Brett stands up, towering over me with an angry expression on his face. "You're making a mistake, Anna. You don't know what's at stake here."

"Yes, I do know exactly what's at stake," I say firmly, my heart pounding in my chest. "I'm staying until the investigation is over. I have nothing to hide and I won't let you or anyone else intimidate me into leaving."

He says nothing as he strides to the door and opens it. Before stepping out, he turns to look at me. "By the way, the gun that was used to kill Madison was found."

He repeats his offer again, telling me that he'll give me two hours to think about it, but I ignore everything he says. All I can think about is the gun in the hands of the police and what it would mean for me if it turns out to be mine.

TWENTY-NINE

After Brett leaves, I find Emily sitting in front of the TV in the bedroom watching the local news. The moment our eyes meet, she feels my pain and jumps to her feet, helping me sit beside her on the bed. After several deep breaths, I tell her what Brett told me.

"How does he know that the gun was found?" she asks.

"He's well connected in this town. He's probably friendly with the police. Maybe they told him."

"And he told you as a way to scare you. But in that case, he must know you had a gun."

"He probably does. Madison managed to enter my cottage, maybe he did as well. Maybe he was curious about who I really am." I bury my face in my hands. "Oh my God," I mutter. "This can't be happening. What if it's my gun?"

"Sweetie, maybe it's not your gun. Just because your gun is missing doesn't one hundred percent mean it's the same one used in the murder. Let's not panic just yet until the police find out whose name is registered to the murder weapon."

"I know, but what if it *is* my gun?" I want to believe it's not mine, but my gut tells me otherwise. If it's mine and they find my fingerprints on it, it's all over. "I can't wait to find out. I have to do something," I say, standing up and walking to the window. "I can't just sit here and wait for them to come and arrest me. Brett made me an offer."

"I know, and don't you dare tell me you're considering it." Emily hands Heather to me.

"I'm... I don't know. But I need to figure out what to do next. I can't just stay here and hope for the best."

Hard, cold evidence is all that counts in the court of law, the only language that's understood. If I'm arrested and go to trial, I could end up being found guilty and be sent to prison for something I didn't do. The thought of being kept away from another child is pure torture.

I gaze down at my daughter, nestled comfortably in my arms, studying her fingers as if she's seeing them for the first time.

Emily grips my arm and waits until I'm looking at her. "I know what you mean. But how do you think that would end? You could end up getting a much worse punishment than you would if you were arrested and convicted right this minute."

I draw in a deep breath, and let it out slowly, trying to think rationally, like an innocent person and not a criminal. "But Brett offered to not only give me the money but also to help me disappear."

Emily gets to her feet and starts to pace the room, her hands buried in her hair. "I don't think this is a good idea, Christa. You could end up in a great deal of trouble. This is not a minor crime. This is murder we're talking about here." She shakes her head. "But if you run, it would be like an admission of guilt. You didn't do this, and if you leave, they'd do everything possible to find you. You're not even sure it's actually your gun, or if it was at all used to kill the neighbor."

"I know. I'm just so confused right now and I'm trying to look at both sides."

I offer Heather my forefinger and she automatically brings it to her lips, but then stops and studies it like she's inspecting its worth. She reaches out both her little hands to grab tighter onto my hand, giggling in delight as her tiny gums clamp down hard onto my skin.

When she pulls away, she babbles something, a mix between a burp and a giggle, and I can't help but smile at her innocence. I watch as she opens her mouth wide and starts to drool. Her cheeks turn bright red and she lets out a loud squeal, demanding my attention once more.

My heart swells with so much love for her I almost can't handle it. It's amazing how much love you can hold for someone you only know for a few months. How much love I still have for my son even after all these years. The idea of being taken away from her kills me inside.

As I look into my daughter's face, I imagine her living life without me. What if without me being there to love her she ends up damaged like Wyatt? No, I cannot let that happen to my child. I need to do everything possible to protect her at all costs.

"You're right, Em. I can't afford to do anything stupid."

I feel foolish for even considering running away. Even if I never get caught, life on the run cannot be easy. I wouldn't want to spend the rest of my life looking over my shoulder, waiting for the law to catch up.

I would never be able to relax, to live, to breathe. To be free enough to look for my son because I definitely will not stop doing that until the day I die.

Deep in thought, Emily twirls a lock of hair around her finger. "We have to do something, though. We can't just sit here and wait for the cops to return."

"I know. The only way out of this is to prove my innocence before they show up again. I need to hurry up and find Wyatt, to prove that he really did this, not me."

"Yes, I think that's a good idea. But what will you tell Brett?"

I'm silent for a moment, thinking about his last words. Before he walked out with his briefcase, he said he'd give me two hours to think about it, and would call me afterwards to ask if I made my decision. If I say yes, he will bring the money to me, and set the wheels in motion to enable me to skip town and end up somewhere safe.

"Perhaps I can delay him? Buy myself some time? As long as I'm still out here, I'll use the time to search for Wyatt and get him to confess to the murder. I'll record him if I have to. As soon as hell broke loose last time, he disappeared. But I know he will reappear again at some point. He always comes back to haunt me, never giving me a chance to forget him." I sigh, my shoulders drooping. "Maybe I should wait and let him show up again on his own."

"I agree." Emily pauses. "I have another idea. Would it help if I take Heather with me back to New York while you take care of all of this? She will be safe there with us and you can focus on this whole thing with no distractions. When you miss her, I can always bring her back anytime."

"That's really sweet of you. But what if Wyatt follows you? What if he kidnaps Heather so he has something to threaten me with?"

"George has a policeman friend. He will keep an eye on us. I'll take very good care of your baby, I promise. I'm her second mother, remember? You don't ever have to worry about her." She gives me a wink and Heather squeals suddenly like she understands our conversation.

"Yes, she's very lucky to have you for a godmother. And I think that's a good idea. Make sure you call me every single night and morning so that she can hear my voice."

Fortunately, Emily is already quite familiar with Heather's

feeding and sleeping patterns, having spent so much time with us.

"Of course, we'll video call you every day so that she can see your face too. I'll also make sure to capture her funny moments on camera."

"Thanks so much, Em." I smile at my baby. "She has enough formula and diapers for another week. I'll pack everything for you."

"Don't worry about a thing. Just focus on taking care of this mess. You'll get through it. I know you will." Heather gurgles in agreement, as if she somehow understands what's going on.

Emily is definitely right. It may be a good idea to get Heather out of this toxic environment. Also, sooner or later, Emily will have to go back to her own child and husband. If the police end up arresting me, I'd have no one I trust to care for Heather. Harper would probably take her, but it's too complicated with Brett in the mix.

Searching for Wyatt with a baby in tow would certainly be stressful for the both of us.

I want this whole mess to be cleared up, then I can raise my daughter in peace. It's a good decision not to take Brett up on his offer. Life on the run is not what I want any child of mine to endure. I need to do what's best for both of us. I need to fight for our freedom.

"When do you plan to leave?" I ask.

"The sooner the better. How about tomorrow?"

THIRTY

I drop Emily and Heather at the airport and head back to the hotel, but I'm only planning to stay one more night. Tomorrow morning, I'll be checking out. I cannot afford to spend another day at the Maryway Hotel, and I will no longer let Emily cover the cost. Since Heather is not with me, I don't need the extra luxury and comfort.

As I drive through Esterford, I keep glancing in the rearview mirror, looking for Wyatt, this time hoping he'll turn up. If he's still in town, he might be watching.

How ironic to think that, before I was accused of murder, I'd been dreading his presence, terrified of him showing up. But now, I need to see him, to face him head on. My desire to get a confession from him dilutes any shred of fear I may have had of him in the past. I'm more afraid of going to prison.

But, of course, now that I need him to come out of hiding, he's not.

I keep driving around town, making endless circles.

Finally, it's 4 p.m., and I've been driving around for an hour and still Wyatt has not shown up. In the end, I return to the hotel, stumped about what to do next. I'm unable to focus on anything.

I sit for a long time on the bed, gazing out the window, watching and waiting for something to happen. I zoom in on every person walking around in the hotel garden, but none of them is Wyatt.

My phone rings as I'm standing up to go to the bathroom, after two hours of doing nothing.

Brett's name flashes across the screen. Taking a deep breath, I answer.

"Hi, Brett," I say.

Yesterday, he called after two hours as he said he would. Instead of shutting down his offer completely, I told him I needed more time. I know I should have rejected the offer immediately, but, for some reason, I just couldn't find it in me to shut down the option just yet. But to Brett, I might as well have said no outright, and he didn't take it well. He was furious and he made threats, but I stood my ground.

"If you don't take this offer right now, Anna, you're going to regret this." I could almost taste his fury through the phone. Then he hung up.

I did not expect to hear from him again, and I still don't have an answer for him.

"Anna, I'm calling to let you know that Harper knows everything. I told her." He pauses for a long time. "I know you were trying to reach her last night. After hearing that you lied to us, she wants nothing to do with you." His voice is flat, unemotional, as my mouth goes dry and my head buzzes with shock.

I can't say I'm surprised that she wants to cut off contact with me. She was good to me and I betrayed her trust. I just can't help wondering how she reacted to him lying to her. I have a feeling that he twisted the truth in some way to favor him. That's if he really did tell her. It could be that he's lying so I back off.

"Stay away from me and my family," Brett warns before I can find my voice, then the phone goes dead.

Maybe the best thing for me to do is to speak to Harper. The least I can do now is apologize for what I did to her. I dial her number twice, but it goes straight to voicemail. When her voice asks me to leave a message, I can only come up with four words that seem far from enough.

"I'm so sorry, Harper." There's not much more to say really. If Brett really did tell her, she will know what I mean. I hang up and focus on my plans.

Given that Brett and Harper are well connected in this town, who knows what they might do to pay me back? I don't expect it from Harper, but Brett is an angry man right now, and he would definitely want me to pay. Just because I didn't accept his offer does not mean he's done with me. For all I know, he might decide to work with the police to make sure I go down for murder. I need to find Wyatt even more urgently before everything starts going wrong.

It's almost seven in the evening now, but I don't care. I put on my coat, grab my purse, and step outside.

As soon as I reach the marble lobby, I hear the whispers. Everyone, both staff and guests, are discussing Madison's murder, and the fact that the murder weapon has been found.

Even though I have nothing to be guilty of, and there's no mention of my name in the conversations, I still feel like everyone is watching my every move and judging me, especially the staff, who might have seen the police when they came to speak to me.

I block them all out, looking neither right nor left, focused on the rotating doors ahead. For now, I'm going for a long walk around town. Maybe if I'm not in my car, Wyatt will find it easier to catch up with me.

So I walk with no destination in mind whatsoever, glancing behind me at every turn. Even in the evening, the town is bustling with activity as people bounce in and out of shops. I wish I could be one of them, carefree and able to just look around, to appreciate this town.

Eventually, I'm too exhausted and still Wyatt has not shown up.

Heading back to the hotel, I realize that maybe I am wasting my time. He might not even be here in town anymore.

If he really killed Madison, he would want to stay as far away as possible and let me take the heat. He's a smart boy and he would never put himself in the line of fire. Instead, he would leave me here to pay for his crime.

He will make sure he's in good hiding, in case the cops catch up with him. This is a small town and it would be easy to track him down if a person knows what they're doing. And the cops certainly do. He may be able to hide from me, but not from them.

He has achieved what he wanted, making me pay for not loving him. If he planted the right evidence, his job here is done and there's no reason for him to hang around. Wherever he is, he must be laughing at me, imagining what I'm doing right now, how desperate I am to find him.

I can't believe he's the boy I used to love, that I cared so much about, that I spent so many wonderful hours together with. I remember him riding the horses in the Austrian village, so happy and carefree.

I thought then he was an innocent child. How could so much have changed since then? It breaks my heart to think that his life is destroyed, and he will never have a normal adulthood with all the damage that he has caused to me and others.

How can somebody move on after committing so many crimes? And with him gone, how can I ever prove that I didn't do what I'm being accused of?

* * *

In the morning, my bags are packed and I'm ready to leave the hotel, but when I check out at reception, the girl behind the counter tells me to wait a second as she has something to give me.

She's about eighteen or nineteen, a brunette with a baby face and a diamond earring in her nose. When she reappears again, she's carrying a gold necklace with a fragile chain hanging from her pointing finger.

"Someone mentioned that you babysit for Harper Wells."

"Well... um, not anymore." I stare at the necklace, recognizing the teardrop pendant immediately. "Is that hers?"

"Yes. One of the maids found it in the room she stayed in last week. I was hoping maybe you could give—"

"Last week?" I pinch the bridge of my nose, confused. "Can you tell me exactly when she stayed here?" I lean against the counter.

"Sh... Sure." After a quick glance behind her, she lowers her gaze to the computer. "She checked in last Friday, and checked out on Sunday afternoon. This looks like an expensive necklace and we would like to return it to her. Unfortunately, we were unable to reach her by phone."

"And you want me to give it to her?"

"Yes, in case you see her."

"Sure, I can do that. I'll be seeing her very soon." I stretch out my hand and open my palm, into which she drops the piece of jewelry.

THIRTY-ONE

An hour has passed since I checked out of the Maryway, and now I'm sitting in my car. The gold necklace dangles from the neck of the rearview mirror, swaying slightly back and forth like it's hypnotizing me.

The receptionist said Harper was in town last weekend and stayed at the hotel for two nights, but that makes no sense at all. Why would she lie about where she was? Why tell us that she was on a retreat when she was really in town?

When we talked on the phone, she made it seem like she returned to town after she heard about Madison's murder. Why did she lie?

I've got to figure out what's going on. The urge to head to her house is strong, but Brett made it clear that he doesn't want me near his family. However, if his work schedule is still the same, he should be at his practice right now.

If Harper is not at the gym, she might be at the house, and we would have time to talk in private.

A single thought keeps running through my mind and it's driving me crazy: what happened that led to Harper and Madison's friendship ending? I need to get the full story so that when I talk to Harper, I have all the facts.

There's one person who might be able to fill in the blanks. I'm hoping Linda, the former nanny, will be willing to answer some questions.

When I arrive at her apartment, I linger in my car and watch the front door of the building. It seems like a long shot that she would be home, but my patience pays off when, an hour later, she steps out from the building.

Exiting the car, I make a beeline for her before she reaches her own car and drives off. My feet slap against the pavement as I run over to her, my breath hitching in my throat. Linda is in her early twenties and has short, dark hair that's sleek and falls just below her ears, and bright, almond-shaped eyes with thick eyebrows sitting above them. She has a petite figure and is dressed casually in a plain olive t-shirt and jeans with frayed hems.

"Linda!" I call out, my voice echoing through the empty street. She turns around and, when she sees me approaching, confusion spreads across her face.

"What are you doing here?" she asks, her voice wary.

"I need to talk to you," I reply, trying to catch my breath. "Can we go somewhere more private?"

"Let me guess. Are you here to warn me about the Wells again, so I don't try to get my job back? I know you went to work for them after I left." Her expression softens. "Don't worry, I'm not pissed or anything. Actually, you did me a favor. After quitting, I found my dream job at the Lotus Spa Center in town. Looking after kids was never my thing." She pauses. "Did you hear about the murder of their neighbor, Madison Baker?"

"Yes. Er... that's kind of what I wanted to talk to you about."

Her eyebrows shoot up. "What would I know about what happened? I no longer work on that street, remember?"

I nod. "Do you mind if we talk someplace quiet?"

"Sure. I'm on my way to work, so we could talk in my car if that's okay with you."

We make our way to her car and settle in, the silence between us stretching taut.

Her car is a small, dark-blue four-door sedan with fogged windows. Its interior is worn and the fabric of the seats is frayed. The steering wheel is slightly off-center with a few scratches on the leather. It smells like stale cigarette smoke mixed with a hint of vanilla air freshener.

I can tell Linda is a little suspicious of me, but I need answers, and I need them now.

"So what do you want to talk to me about?" she asks, cracking open the window enough to let in some fresh air. "I'm not sure what you think I know."

"I just need to ask you some questions about Harper's friendship with Madison."

Her head snaps back. "Wait a minute, you don't think Harper killed Madison, do you? I can tell you right now that it's definitely not her, if that's what you're getting at. That woman is a saint, and I felt terrible for leaving her stranded."

"I know, and I do agree with you. But I need to know everything related to Madison. It might help me track down the person who killed her."

"Right." A deep frown appears between her thick brows. "Why are you so interested in Madison? Did you know her or something?"

"No, I didn't really know her at all. But no one deserves to die the way she did, and like everyone else in this town, I want to make sure the person responsible is brought to justice. I was just curious about her relationship with Harper."

She goes quiet for a while as if thinking about whether to trust me. Then she shrugs. "Their friendship was over about a year ago," she murmurs as she takes a mint from her purse and pops it into her mouth. "They were once very close though. Madison seemed to be quite obsessed with Harper."

"Yes, I got that feeling as well. But I don't understand... What drove them apart? Did you hear anything from the other neighbors?"

"What I heard is that Madison was involved with Harper's husband."

"Madison had an affair with B... Troy?"

Linda clears her throat. "Troy, yes. I didn't want to believe it at first because they seemed to be really good friends, and Harper went on as if life was normal. But then, one night, I came across half-burned photos of Harper and Madison in the fire pit in the backyard." She shakes her head. "I don't think their relationship was healthy, though. Madison was really fixated on Harper. Some of her clothes were almost a carbon copy of Harper's and she often asked me about her whereabouts or what she was doing. It kind of gave me the creeps." Without thinking twice, she tosses the mint wrapper out the window and looks back at me. "I can tell you that Madison wasn't exactly a saint. She had her fair share of enemies. Apparently, she slept with other husbands on the street, so anyone could have wanted her dead. It could be someone else entirely, one of her lovers or their wives. Who knows?" She pauses. "I don't know if it's all true, but that's what people say. That's all I know, though. Now, I really should get going."

"Okay, that's fine. Thank you so much for your time, Linda. I really appreciate it." I open the car door and step out.

As I walk back to my car, my mind races with new information. If those rumors are true about Brett having an affair with Madison, Harper would have motive to kill her, but there are still so many unanswered questions, and I'm going straight to the source to get answers.

THIRTY-TWO

It's eleven when I arrive at Brett and Harper's house. To my surprise, Brett's SUV is parked in the drive, not Harper's car, despite the fact that he should be at work.

I grunt with annoyance as I walk toward their house. I really wanted to have a private conversation with Harper, but maybe it's not a bad thing to speak to Brett either. I'm going to tell him what I suspect and see his reaction.

On my way to the front door, I switch my phone back on, press record, and drop it into the pocket of my coat. Taking a deep breath, I press my finger on the doorbell and wait for someone to answer.

Brett will be furious that I came back to his house when he warned me to stay away from his family. But I don't really care. If he or his wife hold the key to my freedom, I'm not going anywhere.

No one comes to the door. I'm about to ring the bell again, when I notice that it's slightly open. It's strange that they would leave the door like that, especially with Madison's murderer still at large. Maybe they forgot to close it all the way. My heart quickens as I slowly push the door open, trying to make the least amount of noise possible.

"Hello?" I call out, but the only reply is my own voice bouncing off the empty walls. I step forward, my shoes squeaking against the polished wooden floors. I take another step, scanning the hallway. And then I hear a sound coming from somewhere on the ground floor, the kind of sound a person makes when they are in some kind of pain.

As I round the corner and enter the living room, I see Brett sprawled across the couch. His hair is disheveled, and it looks like he hasn't changed out of his clothes in days. When our eyes meet, he lifts his head weakly and drops it again almost instantly.

The pungent aroma of alcohol fills the room, and within seconds, I count at least six empty bottles on the floor scattered around like an army of fallen soldiers.

For a moment, I stand there, searching his face for the man I thought I loved back then, but only seeing the man he has become. His skin is pale and his eyes are puffy and red from alcohol.

"Get out of my house," he spits, but I stand my ground, undeterred by his anger and threats.

"I'm not going anywhere, Brett. I'm not going anywhere until I prove that I'm not the person who killed Madison. I won't let you or anyone else scare me off."

My words seem to amuse him and he lets out a deep laugh that turns into a fit of coughing. When it subsides, he fixes me with a piercing gaze. "I know who killed Madison," he says, but then trails off as if deciding not to divulge further. With some effort, he manages to pull himself into a sitting position.

He sways slowly from side to side as he tries to focus on my face. His hair falls across his forehead, and I can see the sweat on his skin. I can't help but feel a pang of disgust mixed with pity as I watch him struggle to stay upright.

"You know who did it?" My legs buckle as I sit down on the sofa. "First you refuse to tell me where our son is, and now you're telling me you know who killed Madison and watch me get blamed for it? What kind of sick game are you playing, Brett?"

"Let that go already? I told you over and over... the child is dead." He waves his hand, as if shooing a pesky insect away. "He wasn't even my kid." He rises unsteadily, and falls back down onto the couch, next to an empty bottle of gin.

"How could you say that?" I frown. "How could you be so cruel?" I gulp down the disappointment that's filling my chest, realizing once again that the Brett I fell in love with years ago is gone.

"It's the truth." He gets to his feet again, eyes closed tight in an attempt to reorient himself. "A DNA test was done. If you don't want to believe that your child is dead, it's your problem, not mine. I didn't tell you because... I thought I'd spare you the pain of knowing you gave birth to my father's child."

Before I can ask him anything else, he stumbles out of the living room, and I'm standing alone in shock. Is what he's saying true?

Less than a minute later, I hear a car engine roar to life in the driveway. He's driving off drunk—maybe I should run out there and stop him, but I'm paralyzed by the weight of his revelation. My mind is a whirlwind of emotions as I try to process what he's told me.

All these years I wanted to believe we had a baby together. Now it feels like my entire world has been turned upside down.

For the first time ever, I start to question my sanity. I had been married to Brett's father, and he had forced himself on me once before Brett and I got together. Getting into a romantic relationship with Brett was probably a way for me to take back control of my body, and reclaim my power of choice.

Since I didn't want to accept that I was carrying a monster's child, I guess I brainwashed myself into believing that Brett was the father.

Now, suddenly, as the truth hits me like a truck, I start questioning other things I believed. What if my baby really is dead and I also blocked that out? My thoughts swirl around my head like a tornado. I feel like I'm going insane and nothing makes sense anymore.

If that child was really Brett's father's he wouldn't have given it away, since the community believed that children were a blessing and encouraged procreation. What if this entire time, all these years I was searching for a child that's really dead?

I remain on the couch with my thoughts, crying until I'm too exhausted to think or do anything else. This is not my house and I should probably leave, but even if I'm confused about my baby being dead or alive, I'm very sure that I did not kill Madison. I need to stay to protect the child I do have.

I curl up on the sofa and continue the wait. When the edges of a panic attack draw closer, I get off the couch and head to the sliding doors that lead out onto the lake.

As soon as I step outside, my heart starts pounding harder and faster. I'm about to turn around and go back inside when a shift in the air makes the hairs stand up on the back of my neck.

Slowly, I turn around expecting to see Wyatt before me, but instead I find Harper standing there.

Her clothes are as rumpled as Brett's had been, and her face looks gaunt somehow, but the thing that frightens me the most is the hard look in her eyes. She looks nothing like the kind and caring woman I've come to know.

"What are you doing here?" Ice coats her words. I cringe at the hostility in her voice.

My breath comes in gasps as fear snakes around my body. I could be standing in front of a murderer. Despite my fear, something inside of me snaps, and I take a step back, away from the woman I thought was one of the nicest people I had ever met.

Before coming here, I had been wondering whether she really did murder Madison, but now, seeing her standing there with that cold and calculating look, I suddenly know for sure.

"It was you."

THIRTY-THREE

HARPER

I was in high school when my twin sister, Lila, died, and yet I can still remember that night in the abandoned warehouse as if it was yesterday. I vividly remember how she thrashed on the concrete ground, her body writhing in pain and agony, while dark vomit spewed from her lips.

I can still hear the muffled screams that had echoed off the walls, and I can still feel the intense guilt that cut through me, the panic that tasted like metal on my tongue as I tried to save her.

The pain was unbearable as I cradled Lila in my arms, and not even my friends knew how to comfort me. They stood there motionless, unable to do anything but watch, and, when reality set in, they quickly dispersed like shadows in the night before the police arrived, leaving me alone with my twin sister's trembling body.

Lila's beautiful face lost its color as she faded away right before my eyes, and with each breath that left her body, pain seared through me like a branding iron.

When the medics arrived, they could only confirm what I already knew—Lila was gone. My soul shattered into tiny pieces and all I wanted was to take back time and fix things, but instead I had to accept that nothing could be done and all of this was my fault.

It was like my heart had been ripped out of my chest, leaving behind a gaping hole that refused to close, and when Lila's body was taken away in a bag, a part of me went with her.

I felt like I was living a nightmare that I couldn't wake up from. I was desperate for a way out, but there was none. I just had to accept that she was gone. Only a few hours before that, my life was as close to perfect as it could get.

For some kids, high school is a nightmare. As for me, I had the best time of my life, at the beginning at least. I was the IT girl. I had the family wealth, the friends, the parties, and the popularity. I also had a group of friends who followed my every move, and boys who would do anything to be close to me. They called us a clique, but I wouldn't put it that way. We were a group of kids who had each other's backs no matter what. I have to admit that I was feared back then, and I liked it that way.

Initiations into our group were tough, but once you were accepted, you were set for life. We were known to be a little wild, and sometimes we pushed the boundaries too far.

Being in control was everything to me, and I didn't mind breaking a few hearts to maintain it. I was my mother's daughter. She had gone to the same school and was the queen bee in her time, and she taught me well.

Unfortunately, Lila was not as lucky as I was. She was the complete opposite of me, shy and introverted, and she struggled to make friends. It didn't help that I was constantly overshadowing her accomplishments.

To become a member of our club, she also had to go through the initiation process, which I admit was a bit harsh on her. I wanted to toughen her up, to make her more like me. But it didn't work out that way.

I never thought that one day in July, something would

happen that would turn my world upside down. That summer night, my friends and I decided to throw a party in an abandoned warehouse. I invited Lila and a few other girls who failed our initiation to attend. It was their last chance to prove themselves to us.

I felt compelled to treat my sister like everyone else, scared I'd lose my friends if I showed favoritism.

During the party, we dared them to drink a highly alcoholic concoction that we had made for the occasion. Some of the girls refused and left the party. Lila was hesitant at first, but eventually succumbed to the pressure of wanting to be accepted by us. That's when things took a turn for the worse.

Lila had a severe allergic reaction to the drink we had given her, and she ended up dying in my arms. That night, I lost not only my sister but also a part of myself, the part of me I used to find pride in.

I killed my sister and I made myself a promise that I would spend the rest of my life doing enough good to make up for it, to make amends for the terrible mistake I had made.

I became a shadow of my former self, spending most of my days volunteering at shelters and soup kitchens, trying to make a difference. In college, I even studied social work, hoping to help others avoid the same fate as my sister.

The moment I met Troy, in front of my university, and he helped me distribute the sandwiches, I could instantly see that we shared the same passion for helping people, and it didn't take long before we fell in love. He was patient and understanding, listening to my story without judgment. He knew about my past, but he never looked down on me for it. He also didn't care about the age gap between us, and neither did I. We were soulmates.

We dated only for a short time and got married a week before I turned nineteen. My mother was livid and threatened to disown me. Hearing her say that hurt deeply, especially since she was all I had. My father had divorced her after Lila died and started a new life with another woman, forgetting about us.

Two years after Troy and I were married, Mom died and I was shocked to find that she'd left me a letter. In it, she wrote about how sorry she was for everything she had done, how she regretted forcing me to toughen up and how much she admired the good work that I was doing.

Reading that letter was cathartic for me. I finally felt like I was being released from the burden of my past. All the money she left me was nothing compared to the closure I received through her last words to me.

She left me enough money that allowed me the freedom to never work if I chose not to. I started charities, helped the homeless and the poor. The more I helped, the more I wanted to do. The satisfaction and joy that came with being there for others was something I had never experienced before, and I realized that this was my true calling. For the first time in my life, I felt truly happy. I had a wonderful husband who I was crazy about and, later, two daughters who were the light of my life.

Everything was perfect. Until it wasn't.

Some people say cheating is not really cheating if it's only a kiss. To me, what Troy and Madison did felt like a betrayal of all the trust we had built over the years. I could feel the anger and hurt boiling inside of me, and I didn't know how to handle it.

Troy promised me that it was nothing, that Madison was drunk and was the one who came on to him. I chose to believe him, but Madison no longer felt like a true friend. She was someone I confided in, someone I trusted, and now that trust was broken. The betrayal lingered in my mind, festering like a wound that refused to heal.

But after a few painful months, life went back to normal and I continued my good work. When Christa showed up on our doorstep, all I saw was a woman who needed help, devastated after her husband's death. I wanted to be there for her, and I needed her after my nanny left suddenly.

But then Madison came to me with all her suspicions. She didn't trust Christa. But the problem was, I didn't trust Madison either. To be honest, I had never forgiven her or Troy for what they did to me. My anger and hurt still simmered just beneath the surface, threatening to boil over at any moment.

The day she came to tell me she suspected something was going on between Troy and Christa, I still didn't believe her, but I wanted to play it safe. So I lied that I was going on a retreat out of town. Instead, I checked into the Maryway and took a taxi back to the house in the evening.

While Christa was in the house taking care of the kids and making dinner, I snuck into her cottage and hid to wait until Troy came home from work. Curious about who the woman working for me really was, I found myself snooping around her belongings, searching for any evidence that showed me she could not be trusted.

That's when I found the gun under her mattress. I could not understand why she would bring a deadly weapon into my home and not say anything. I wrapped one of her scarfs around the gun and put it in my purse, not really sure what to do about it yet. When I saw Troy's car pull up the driveway, with a sick feeling in my stomach, I quickly left the cottage and hid outside in the bushes where I was able to see them in the kitchen.

I watched as they sat down at the kitchen table, which was strange because I did not expect them to have dinner together while I was away. What also sprung out to me immediately was that they were talking like they knew each other, even though Troy rarely said a word to her when I was around.

From their body language, I noticed that they were arguing about something. Troy did what he normally did when he was upset, which is rub a finger vigorously under his nose like he was trying to push away a bad smell.

I wanted to go to the kitchen window to hear what they were saying, but I didn't want to risk being seen.

A few minutes later, while I was still hiding in the shadows trying to understand what must have happened between them, I watched my husband grab Christa, who was carrying Heather, by the arm and push her out of the house before slamming the door shut. My stomach filled with acid.

I knew my husband to be a gentle man, and I had never seen him act with such force before, and definitely not toward a woman holding a baby. I remained frozen in place, watching as Troy returned to the kitchen. Then I saw Madison appear as though out of nowhere. She and Troy also had a conversation that looked heated. Then I saw him reach for her, pulling her close, and I felt my heart explode inside my chest.

THIRTY-FOUR

When Troy pulled Madison toward him, about to kiss her, something shifted inside me and I turned away. I couldn't bear to watch as the man I loved betrayed me again. I couldn't watch the woman I'd once called a friend let me down one more time.

As I walked away, the girl I had left behind in high school suddenly resurfaced, and I felt a surge of anger and disgust wash over me.

It became clear to me then why Madison was trying to make me doubt Christa: she was still having an affair with my husband and needed some way to mask their wrongdoing. I had seen enough. Without thinking about consequences, I stormed off my property and went to hide in the foliage in Madison's garden, waiting for her to come home.

I silently prayed she wasn't planning on staying at my home with my husband and children. Luckily, she didn't, and, as soon as she entered her house, I rushed up to the door. She was not expecting me, of course, because I was supposed to be away, but I did not give her a chance to say a word.

I shoved her back into the house, and the moment the door

closed behind me, I pulled out the gun and aimed it at her head. When I confronted her about what happened, she had the nerve to deny it, even with a gun about to blow her brains out.

"There's nothing going on between us, I swear." Her hands shook as she held them up in surrender. "I was confronting Troy about… about Christa. Nothing happened."

"Don't you lie to me," I spat out through gritted teeth. "I know he kissed you." I didn't stay long enough to see, but I know it happened. "Do you think I'm an idiot? Did you think you can just go on hurting people without consequences?"

"Troy and I did not kiss. I told you I'll never do that to you again." She was crying now, but I wasn't moved. "Please hear me out. You have to listen to me."

"You really expect me to listen to the woman who wants to steal my life? You don't think I see what you're doing? I know you want to be me, Madison. And now you're set on taking my husband."

"I'm not looking to take your husband—or your life. I'm honestly not interested in Troy… at all. You should be more concerned about your nanny. She's the one who's been deceiving you. She lied to get into your home."

"What the hell do you mean?"

"She knows Troy. They grew up together in Bluefort. They had a baby together. They—"

"Stop lying to me." As hard as my tone was, my fingers weakened around the gun.

"I swear, I'm telling the truth." With one hand raised in defense, she dug into her back pocket and pulled out her phone, tossing it onto a chair close to where I stood. "Take a look at it," she said. "There are messages in there from Jude, the PI I hired to investigate Christa. There's a lot more than meets the eye with that woman." I only glanced at the phone, but didn't pick it up as Madison continued. "The last family she worked for as a nanny is dead. She probably killed them. You could have a murderer living in your house right now."

"That's ridiculous." Blood pounded in my ears, but I could feel my grip on the gun slipping. "You're just trying to get out of this. You're having an affair with my husband and you won't get away with it. I won't let you." My grip on the firearm tightened again, but I was now aiming at her chest instead of her head.

"Harper, I'm being honest—can't you see? I'm only trying to look out for you. You're like a sister to me." Madison's voice was desperate, and fear swirled in the depths of her eyes.

"I don't believe a word you're saying."

As I raised the gun, my finger trembling on the trigger, she darted forward with a desperate cry. Her outstretched hands clamped down on mine and I felt her weight pushing against me as she tried to wrench the weapon away.

We landed on the floor, and we grappled violently until the gun fired unexpectedly.

I felt something warm and wet splatter across my face, and dropped to my knees to find Madison lying motionless on the floor with a pool of deep-red liquid surrounding her.

I didn't mean to kill her that night. I only meant to scare her. But, she died, and I had to do something about it or end up in prison. As I stared down at Madison's motionless body, I was still sure that she was accusing Christa of all those things because she wanted to distract attention from the affair she was having with my husband.

If the police showed up and uncovered the truth of why we were no longer friends, they would know I had a motive to take her life. So instead of calling them, I had to save myself.

Choosing the person to pin the crime on was easy. It would be the person whose gun was used to shoot Madison.

If there was a chance that Christa really did kill her previous employers, then she was capable of killing Madison as well. She would be the first person the cops would suspect.

My plan was foolproof. All I had to do was set up the evidence and make it look like Christa did it.

Before I put my plan into action, I picked up Madison's phone to see if she was telling the truth.

THIRTY-FIVE

CHRISTA

"You murdered Madison," I repeat, my voice low and measured. I'm hoping the truth will catch her off guard before she has a chance to deny it, to prepare for a response.

Her expression falters for a fraction of a second, and I know I've hit a nerve.

The woman before me is a stranger now. Her bloodshot eyes are swollen and full of rage, her skin pale, her red lips puckered into a hard line. Right now, she definitely looks like someone who would be capable of murder.

I watch as she takes a step back, almost stumbling at the weight of my words as though they have hit her with physical force. She steadies herself, but I can see the faint tremble in her hands.

Her expression changes from shock to anger. "How dare you accuse me of such a terrible thing when it was your gun that was used—" she catches herself and the tip of her nose turns bright red.

Bingo.

"You know I own a gun," I whisper. Even as rage pumps through my veins, I manage to crack a victorious smile. "And how exactly do you know that it's the murder weapon, Harper? As far as I know, the police haven't released that information to the public. Unless, of course, you stole it and used it. And now you're waiting for the police to charge me with murder while you walk away scot-free. I think it was also you who stole my scarf and left it at the crime scene so that I'd be the prime suspect."

"You're crazy," she shouts, but, in the space between her words, I hear it: a slight but distinct tremble, a hint of fear, a quiver in her voice that betrays her. "I have nothing to do with what happened to Madison."

"You're lying and we both know it." My throat tightens with anger as I take a step closer to her.

"Really?" She laughs out loud. "You... you are the liar here. You walked into my house and pretended to be someone you are not. You took advantage of my kindness."

Her eyes burn through me with a fiery intensity, and the hairs on the back of my neck stand up. Even her voice has changed, raspy and deep, almost like that of a man's. Her nostrils flare like an angry bull's, her breath labored and heavy.

I force myself to stay still, not daring to look away. This is the moment of truth, the moment when everything will be revealed. I won't walk away until I know the truth.

The recording app on my phone is running, catching every word that comes out of her mouth. As soon as I'm out of here, I'm taking the evidence straight to the police. All I need is for her to confess, to admit what she did.

"What I did is nothing compared to the crime you committed. I didn't murder Madison, you did. How could you live with yourself knowing that you're about to be responsible for sending someone to prison for something they didn't do?" I can barely force the words out, my throat thick with emotion. "I'm a mother and you are prepared to destroy my life and take me away from my child."

This time, she averts her gaze, but just for a moment before the guilt is replaced with a look of steely resolve. "I don't know what you're talking about." Her voice is low and dangerous. "I didn't kill anyone."

She's trying hard to cover up her unraveling emotions and act as if she's in control, but I can see through her facade.

"Stop lying to me, Harper." I take another brave step forward. "You are a murderer, and you deserve to spend the rest of your life behind bars for what you've done."

At my accusatory words, Harper's face twists into a mask of fury. "You have no proof," she growls. Her hands ball into fists at her sides as she struggles to keep her composure. "You can't walk into my house uninvited and accuse me of murder. Why would I ever hurt Madison? She was my friend." As she speaks, fake tears make their way down her face, but I can see the glimmer of satisfaction in her eyes. She's enjoying this, reveling in the chance to manipulate the situation to her advantage.

"She *used* to be your friend," I remind her, dipping my head to one side. "I know now that the reason you were not friends anymore is because she was involved with your husband. And I have a feeling it happened again. If you ask me, that's a pretty big motive for murder."

I'm ready to hurl everything and anything at her to break her resistance, to knock her off guard and force her to tell me the truth.

"You don't know what you're talking about." She stumbles backward toward a beige velvet armchair close to the door, then sinks into it.

Her hands shake on the armrests as they clutch them so tight that her knuckles turn white. The fear etched on her face is palpable and her gaze darts around the room, as if searching for a way out, but there is no escape from the truth.

Out of nowhere, I feel a twinge of sympathy. But then I

remember what she did to me, and what would happen if she gets away with murder.

Time seems to stands still as we stare at each other until she lets out a deep breath, pushing her fingers through her hair. A desperate groan escapes her lips before her head drops back against the chair in defeat. But she says nothing.

"Admit it, Harper. You killed Madison because she had an affair with your husband and now you want to pin it on me. You can't do this. I'm an innocent person."

"You? Innocent?" She laughs, a mocking sound that echoes through the room and chills me to the bone. "No, sweetie. You're no angel. You're a criminal and a liar who spun me a sob tale of your husband dying and being left homeless with your baby. Madison told me everything about you. The truth is, you walked into my house because you were after my husband. When exactly did you plan on telling me that you and my husband knew each other... that you have a child together?"

"We don't... I..." I swallow the knot in my throat. It still so hard to accept that my baby was not Brett's. "I never wanted your husband. It's not what you think."

"Not what I think, or what I know? The truth is that you both grew up in a cult in some village. You were in a relationship, and you had a child together." She inhales sharply. "I didn't want to believe it, you know? I didn't want to believe that my husband is a liar. That's why I didn't talk to him about it until today. But now that I know, he will pay for what he did to me and our family. For what you did, you also deserve everything that's coming to you."

That's it. Surely, that's a confession. But my satisfaction is diluted by the pain unfolding on her face. Feeling suddenly exhausted, I flop down onto the couch.

"Believe it or not, I never wanted to destroy your marriage, Harper. I didn't mean to hurt you. It must be hard for you to accept that now, after everything, but it's true. I came here because I wanted him to tell me where my child is."

"You think I'm stupid, don't you?" Her shoulders heave with mirth.

"No, not at all. But I know Madison is dead and you killed her. The police need to know." I start to make my way toward the door and she jumps from the armchair and surges forward, catching me off guard with her speed and strength.

For a small woman she's surprisingly strong. As she wrestles for me not to step out of the door, her fingers are tight around my arms, shoving me back into the room before slamming the door shut. Then she runs to the fireplace and grabs the poker, swinging it wildly in my direction, ready to attack me if I dare leave the room.

"You're not going anywhere," she spits, her eyes blazing with fury. "I will not allow you to destroy my life again. I'll kill you if I have to."

THIRTY-SIX

"You can't do this, Harper." I back away, my heart pounding as I search for a way out. But she's between me and the door. "I won't go to prison. I didn't kill anyone."

"Is that so? Now how am I supposed to know that?" She raises an eyebrow. "From what I heard, the last family you worked for ended up dead. You killed them, didn't you?"

I shake my head, clenching my lips together. "I did not kill them, and if you followed the case online, you will know that the right person... the person who committed the murders... is in prison."

"And he's your boyfriend. He probably took the fall to protect you."

I stand tall and take a step toward her, no longer scared. "I'm not like you, Harper. I would never be able to live with myself if someone went to jail for something I did. You killed Madison, and that stain will never go away, regardless of who ends up in prison."

"What evidence do you have that I did it? None. I'm innocent, Christa."

"Well, then, if you're so sure of your innocence, prove it and let me out of here."

I try to pass by her again, but am quickly met with a fierce sting on my side. Wincing, I grab onto my stomach as a burst of agony shoots through me.

"I said, you're not going anywhere," she repeats with more force than before.

Gritting my teeth together, I straighten up and try again to get past her, but there's murder in her eyes. The darkness in her gaze leaves me cold. She's not going to let me go. I suppose we all have a shadowy side that reveals itself when we are pushed to our limits. Harper is no exception, and her demeanor tells me that she'll do whatever it takes to keep me from leaving with information that could incriminate her.

But I'll also do whatever it takes to stay out of prison. I will not let anyone keep me from another one of my children. If she wants to fight, I'm ready.

When she swings at me again, I duck and step forward, shoving her hard against the door so much that she loses her breath. With her back against the door, she slides to the floor. For a moment I fear she cannot breathe and I'm tempted to go and help her. But then she starts crying, her wails echoing throughout the room.

"I didn't mean to... It was an accident," she chokes out between sobs.

Her words are barely audible over her cries, but they're unmistakable. And I'm close enough for my phone to record them as evidence for the police.

"If it was a mistake, then we have to tell the police that. I can talk to them. Together, we can make them understand. I know you're a good person, Harper. You can—"

"No," she shouts, the anger returning, her violent streak back as she kicks her leg out hard and trips me. I stumble backward, landing hard on the floor.

She takes advantage of this and right away she's on top of me. Her nails dig into my skin as she tries to hold me down.

Without warning, she takes a handful of my hair and slams the back of my skull onto the hardwood. "I won't let you ruin my life," she shouts, her voice growing louder with each blow.

Pain radiates through my head and a red-hot rage pulses through my veins. I grab her wrists, fighting to pry her fingers away from my scalp, but she won't let go.

She's like a dog with a bone and won't back down. Blood rushes to my ears and stars begin to swim in my vision.

I'm so close to succumbing to her, to surrendering my safety and freedom when something inside me shifts. I know my nose is bleeding, my lip is split, and my body is bruised, but I'm far from broken.

With a fierce determination, I manage to untangle her fingers and shove her off of me. I barely have time to stand before she's charging at me again. I step to the side, narrowly avoiding her attack and she crashes into the wall.

Grabbing the chance, I dash for the door, only to find it locked. How did she lock it without me seeing her? Panting, and with my head pounding, I turn to face her again to find that she has recovered and is wielding the poker again.

"You will not go to the police." She has blood on her lip. Is it mine or hers?

"Fine." I raise up my hands and step back toward the open glass doors leading out onto the balcony as she continues to shove the tip of the poker in my direction. "I won't go to the cops, but you have to turn yourself in. You need to end this now."

I turn my head slightly to look at the lake behind me, and my stomach drops. I can't swim and Harper knows that.

"No one is going to the police. Not you, and not me. No one even knows this conversation happened."

She raises the poker, and, instinctively, I raise my arms to protect them from the strike. It doesn't stop Harper from slamming it against my hands. Crying out, I bring them to my chest, cradling them against my body. Without giving me a chance to recover, the next blow to one side of my head sends me reeling.

My vision blurs as I stumble backward, but I'm able to catch myself before I fall too far. Harper then thrusts the poker at my chest and draws it back, leaving a nasty cut.

"That's enough, Harper." I'm still shaking and can barely hold a thought in my head. "Please, stop this before you do something you'll regret." I clutch my head with both hands, blood dripping down my temple.

My words stop her and she drops the poker. She steps back, her gaze heavy with a mix of fear and hatred. She may have let go of the poker, but she's not done with me. I can't even move away from her anymore because I'm dangerously close to the edge of the dock.

"The only thing I will regret is if I let you walk out of here alive," she snarls, her voice cracking with emotion. Then, before I know it, she plants both hands on my chest and shoves me.

With a scream, my feet slip from underneath me and I'm thrown backward into the lake. My body hits the cold water with a loud splash.

Overcome by fear and pain, I struggle to stay above the water. The cold liquid fills my nose, eyes, mouth, and ears. Panic surges through my body like an electric bolt, and I struggle to stay afloat as my weakened limbs tremble from fatigue and pain. The frigid temperatures begin to sap away my energy. With each passing second, I sink deeper into the abyss. Every effort to keep my head above water is in vain.

For the first time since I was a child, I wish I had pushed past my anxiety and learned to swim. My only chance of survival is someone rescuing me, but the dock is facing away from the street, and I doubt anyone knows what happened.

More dirty water floods my nose and mouth, and I can feel

my strength fading. I'm pulled farther and farther away, and soon I'm too weak to even keep my head above the surface.

Through my half-closed lids, I see Harper watching from above for a few seconds before she disappears out of sight, leaving me alone in the darkness.

I take a deep breath of the lake water, and it rips through my chest. Everything goes black as I'm pulled under. As my world becomes smaller and darker, death feels closer than ever.

My chest tightens as I attempt to scream for help but no sound comes out. Deep into the lake I go, away from everyone who could save me.

The last thing I see before accepting my fate is my daughter's face.

THIRTY-SEVEN

I wake up to find my hospital room dim, lit only by moonlight streaming in from the window. A heavy weight is pressing down on me, like I'm being pushed into the small bed.

Even though the nurse gave me pain meds only an hour ago, before she wished me a goodnight, pain still racks my body. My head hurts. My hands hurt. My chest hurts. It feels like I'm constantly struggling against pain that makes it hard for me to sleep again.

"Hi," someone whispers and I turn slowly to look at my side.

As soon as I see him, fear rises in my chest. He's here. He found me. I shut my eyes, wishing this is all a nightmare. Maybe I did drown in the lake and this is a dream. But when I look again, he's still there, perched by the side of my bed, wearing a black baseball cap.

I try to shift away, to put more distance between us, but I can't move. I'm too weak and in too much pain.

"You don't have to be afraid of me." Wyatt places a hand on my arm. "I just want to talk to you."

I hold my breath, waiting for what comes next, wondering

what would happen if I reach out for the bell that will alert the nurses that I need help.

"What do you want?" I whisper.

Maybe he watched me fall into that lake and saw that I survived. Is he here to finish what the water couldn't? But then he does something unexpected—he reaches out to hold my bandaged hand. He doesn't make a single move to hurt me.

"I wanted to see if you're okay." His voice is soft and gentle, and there are tears in his eyes.

Uncertain about whether he's trying to manipulate me, I pull my hand away. His behavior can be so erratic, and it's hard to tell when the dark part of him might take over again.

"What are you doing here? What do you want from me? I'm not your mom, Wyatt. You have to accept that."

He leans his head a bit closer to mine. "It was me who dragged you out of the water."

When I arrived at the hospital in an ambulance, thanks to almost drowning and the deadly blow to my head, I was so confused and disoriented that I couldn't remember what had happened since I was pushed into the lake.

The paramedics said they found me on the shore unconscious, but they had no idea who had pulled me out of the water, or if I'd crawled out on my own. When they revived me, I had no recollection either of how I got there.

But now I suddenly do. I remember the strong grip on my arm, someone hauling me out of the lake. I sputtered water as the person pressed their hands on my chest to get me to breathe again. But I was barely awake when my rescuer disappeared, and, before I knew it, I fell unconscious again.

"It was you... You saved my life?" My voice is hoarse as I stare at the boy in front of me.

"I saw that woman push you into the water. I called the ambulance for you, and the cops for her. I told them what she did. She killed that neighbor."

Shock cuts through me as I digest his words. "You know? How?"

"Yes." He drops his head. "I was there the night it happened. I have videos and everything. I sent it all to the cops." He looks up again. "I should have come forward earlier to tell them you didn't do it."

"Why didn't you?" It's a rhetorical question because I know why he didn't, and he soon confirms it.

"I wanted you to suffer. You didn't want to be my mother, so I was mad. That's why I sent the cops that photo of you arguing with the dead woman." He pauses. "I'm sorry."

Of course he knows everything. If he was always stalking me, he would've seen it all. He could have come forward and saved me a lot of pain and heartache, but he didn't. But then he went and did something I never expected. He pulled me out of that water and called for help.

He could have left me to die, to punish me. I'm not sure what it all means. What if this fuels his obsession with me? What if he thinks that, since he saved my life, I owe him?

"Thank you, Wyatt. But I'm still not your mother. The DNA—"

"Yeah." He yanks off his baseball cap and runs a hand over his head before placing it back on again. "It's fine. I accept it now."

I don't know what to say, or how to react to this new change in his personality. Is he playing some kind of game with me? What if I blink and he's back to his old ways?

"Look, I'm sorry for what I did. I was angry because you didn't care about me anymore," he whispers through his sobs.

"I cared, Wyatt. You know I did. And that's why I came to see you that day at the school. I cared about you so much that I didn't want to believe you did those horrible things. But then you did and said more things that terrified me."

"I know." He wipes his eyes with his sleeve. "I don't want to be that person. I don't want to do bad things anymore. I just couldn't stop myself."

Pushing past my fears and hurts, I reach for his hand, clasping it. This boy has made my life hell, but in the end he's here. He's saved my life and has given me a second chance to be with my daughter.

"You have to get help," I plead with him.

"I know." He lets out a deep sigh. "I'm going to the police. I'm going to tell them everything."

"You are?" My heart leaps into my throat. I didn't expect that at all.

Now that he has finally done the right thing in the end, I want to tell him to run and promise to be a different person. To tell him that the police do not need to know what he did, as long as he never does it again, but I can't do it. Ultimately, he did kill somebody and it's not my place to make those kinds of decisions for him. If I tell him right now not to come forward and at some point in the future he harms somebody else, I'd be responsible.

"I just want you to do the right thing," I say instead.

"I will." He rises to his feet. "I also came to tell you that I accept it... that you're not my mom biologically. But in my heart, you are. I saved your life because I love you and I'm sorry. Goodbye, Christa."

"Wyatt," I call as he walks to the door. "How did you get into the cottage even though all the doors and windows were locked?" It's a question that has been tormenting me since the day he showed up.

He turns around, his hand on the doorknob. "I snuck into the main house once when Harper left the door open, and stole the spare key hanging on the hook in the kitchen."

"But how? It was never missing."

"Yes, you're right. That's because I later replaced it with a fake key that looked almost identical. I thought it would be a while before anyone noticed."

"You stole the key and replaced it with a fake one?" My lips part in disbelief. Here I was thinking that keeping the spare key with me would keep us safe, but, in reality, it was just a ruse. I never thought it necessary to test it, to make sure it was genuine.

My mind races with all the many more times he could have snuck into my cottage undetected, and I shudder at the thought.

Wyatt's shoulders slump forward. "I'm really sorry, Christa. I never meant to hurt you. You won't see me again."

With that, he walks out of the room and I continue to watch the closed door, my heart feeling heavy with both sadness and relief. It's over.

In the morning, I'm still thinking about what happened last night, wondering if I dreamed it all. It's only when I look at the chair next to the bed and notice a small passport photo that I know Wyatt was really here. It's the photo I had given him in Austria when child protective services were taking him away. The photo I gave him so he would never forget about me.

I reach for it, holding it between my fingers. Even if I was worried that what he said was not true, this is a confirmation. This could be a sign that he's really letting me go.

Later in the afternoon, when Emily arrives in town and comes to see me with Heather, I'm still troubled. But I hold my baby to myself, weeping softly into her hair as Emily watches on.

Finally, she smiles down at me. "I'm so happy you're okay. I'll forever be grateful to the person who saved you."

"It was Wyatt." I rest my chin on top of Heather's head. "He's the person who pulled me out of the water. He tried to save me, but I fell unconscious again. Luckily, he had called for help."

Emily's fingers fly to her lips, and her eyes widen with

shock. "Are you sure about this? How... How do you know it was him?"

"I saw him yesterday," I say. "He was here last night."

"What? Did you call the police?"

"No. He saved me, Em. At first, I thought he was going to hurt me, but then he told me what he did for me. Apparently, he also sent evidence to the police that confirms that Harper did kill Madison. He was there the night of the murder."

Emily breathes out as she sinks into the chair where Wyatt had been sitting just a few hours ago. "I don't know what to say."

"I didn't either. Here's another shocker." I inhale deeply before continuing. "He said he has come to terms with me not being his mom." I motion toward the picture on the nightstand next to me. "He left that behind. I gave it to him when we were in Austria."

"So you think this is really over?" Emily nods slowly, her gaze flicking between me and the photo. "You think he will really go away?"

"I really don't know. He didn't hang around long enough for me to find out exactly what his next plans are, but it looked like he genuinely wants to change... to move on."

"Honestly, Christa, I'm not sure whether to believe that. Too much has happened."

I say nothing, because part of me feels the same way she does.

That evening, the sheriff surprises me with a visit.

After greeting me, he gets straight to the point. "I'm sure you heard that we found the gun that was used to kill Madison Baker? We were told it's yours."

Immediately, an image of my handgun flashes through my

mind, a semi-automatic with a sleek black finish and a white rubberized grip that prevents slipping and helps with aiming.

"Yes, sir, I think it was. It had gone missing." There's no point in lying now. I feel myself shrink back into the bed. What if the evidence was not enough to lead to Harper's arrest, and he's here to arrest me? "But I didn't do it. I didn't kill that woman."

"I believe you," he says with a reassuring smile.

"Thank you." Relief washes over me, but I'm still on tenterhooks.

"Why did you lie to us about the gun?" He walks over to the window. "You told us your gun was in New York."

"Because I suspected I was being set up."

He turns away from the window and pushes his hands into his pockets. "Looks like you were right about that, but wrong about who was doing it. I wanted to let you know that Harper Wells is in custody. We found her fingerprints on the gun, and she confessed to the murder. Not that she had a choice, we were provided with overwhelming evidence against her. That boy you were afraid of filled in the blanks that Harper left out." He removes his hands from his pockets and meets my gaze. "But he also confessed to the two murders you suspected him of committing, the nanny and the foster mother, Judy Adams."

My heart races as I process the news, but it also breaks for Wyatt. "What will happen to him now?"

"It's hard to say since one of the murders occurred outside the borders of this country. There's a chance he will be sent back to Austria to be detained there, but there's still the issue of the murder he confessed to committing in the United States that makes it more complicated. It's all up in the air at the moment, I'm afraid." The sheriff sighs. "He's one troubled kid and he needs help, that much is clear. Regardless of what happens, I'll do my best to make sure he gets it." He pauses to look at me. "There's something else you should know, Miss Rogers."

I frown and then blink several times. "Okay. What is it?"

He hesitates for a moment before breaking the news, his voice low and heavy with sorrow. "Troy Wells was involved in a deadly car accident yesterday. He was driving under the influence of alcohol and lost control of his car. He survived, but I hear his condition is very critical."

The words land like a punch and my hands fly to my mouth, muffling a gasp that escapes me nonetheless. The world narrows around us, collapsing into this devastating revelation. "You think he might not make it?"

"The doctors are doing everything they can, but it's not looking good." His voice is heavy with sympathy. "He's in a coma right now."

Even though there's nothing left between Brett and me, and he proved himself not to be the person I used to know, I'm overcome with a sadness so intense it feels like a physical weight on my chest. I feel especially sad for the twins who already have one parent behind bars, and if Brett doesn't make it, they could end up being orphans.

"Oh my God," I whisper, my voice choked with emotion. "Does Harper know?" I'm not even sure why I care given what she did to me, but I can't help the question.

The sheriff nods. "Yes, she was informed, but she didn't show much of a reaction. I apologize again for everything that happened to you. If there's anything we can do, please let us know."

Unable to get any more words out, I nod and watch him walk to the door.

* * *

Brett's hospital room is small and sterile, the beeping of machines providing a soundtrack. The smell of antiseptic hangs in the air and light streams in from the window, casting a glow on his pale face. I stand at the foot of his bed, unsure of what to say or do. Three days after being discharged from the hospital, I'm back again.

Even though doctors feared that Brett was not going to wake up, he has. I never thought I'd see him again, but last night I received a call that he wanted to see me.

He looks so much smaller now, lying there in the hospital bed with tubes and wires attached to him. His once strong and muscular body is now frail and fragile.

Seeing him in such a vulnerable state, which reminds me of the man he used to be, I can't find it in me to hold onto the anger and resentment that I had been carrying toward him for so long. Instead, all I feel is a deep sadness.

I can't help but think about the last time I saw him before leaving the community.

It was on the morning I escaped the cult, and we had all had breakfast together as one big, unhappy family. I remember how he had looked at me that morning, like he knew what I was up to. But he couldn't ask me because we were forbidden from talking to each other. Later that morning, when I snuck into Emily's parents' delivery truck and we drove off, I never thought I'd see him again. But here we are.

He wakes up as soon as I sit down next to him, and gives me a weak smile. "Hey," he whispers, his voice barely audible.

To avoid reaching out to touch him, I tuck my hands underneath my thighs. "Hey," I reply, my voice just as soft. "How are you feeling?"

Brett takes a deep breath before answering. "Like shit, to be honest. But I'm alive, so that's something."

I nod, unsure of what else to say. It's strange being here with him after everything that happened. "You wanted to see me?"

"I'm sorry," he says suddenly, his gaze locking onto mine. "For everything. For what I did to you."

I'm taken aback by his apology. It's not what I expected to hear from him, especially in his current condition. "It's okay," I reply, trying to sound as reassuring as possible. "I'm trying to move on, and I hope you can too."

Brett shakes his head. "I can't move on until I make things right. I know I hurt you, and I want to make it up to you. I should have protected you from them." He cringes as he swallows hard. "I should have stopped them from sending you away. I just didn't... I was a coward. I was afraid of him."

I nod sadly. "I know. Me too. Running away was the hardest thing I ever did. For years, I lived in fear. I thought they would find me and—"

"But they didn't. You were braver than all of us. You are a survivor." His eyes well up and I can see the pain etched across his face. "I never expected to see you again. When you showed up to work for us, I thought it was you—"

"You did? You recognized me?"

"At some deep level, but I didn't want to admit it to myself, even when the signs were there. Let's just say maybe I didn't want it to be true. So, I talked myself into believing I was wrong, that it was all in my head. I'm so sorry for how I treated you when you told me who you are. I was scared to lose everything. But that isn't an excuse for being a jerk. I just wanted to believe that my past was behind me and had not come back to haunt me." He blinks several times. "Sorry, I didn't mean you came back to haunt me. I meant the memories, the guilt, the shame. Admitting it was you would have brought back everything. Every memory, every feeling, every regret. I was not ready."

I nod, understanding his struggle. "It's okay. I know what you mean. But we can't keep running away from our past, Brett. We have to face it head on and deal with it, no matter how painful it is."

"Yeah, I know now that I can't run away from it forever."

There's a moment of silence between us, and I can feel the tension rising. It's strange being alone with him like this, all our history between us.

His chest heaves as he takes another deep breath. "I'm also very sorry for what Harper tried to do to you... framing you for murder." He pauses. "Shortly before you arrived at the house, she admitted it to me. But she's my wife. I didn't want her to go to prison. But she tried to kill you as well and that's unforgivable. And I feel partly guilty. If I had confronted my fears of the past, it would not have come that far. Actually, everything that happened is because of me. What Harper did... it was out of jealousy. I was unfaithful in our marriage and I guess she never forgave me."

"Or Madison," I add. "I heard about it. But why did you do it?"

Brett looks away from me, but not before I see the shame etched on his face. "I really don't know. I asked myself that question a million times. Self-sabotage, I guess. I had everything I wanted, a beautiful wife, two beautiful children, and a successful career. Maybe I didn't think I deserved it all." He pauses, taking a moment to collect his thoughts. "If I had not been so stupid as to kiss Madison, she would probably be alive, and my wife would not be behind bars right now." His brow forms deep wrinkles. "To be honest, I actually thought Madison planned the whole thing."

"What do you mean?"

"I thought she died by suicide and somehow made it look like a murder, with the help of someone, of course... to frame me."

My eyebrows shoot up. "But why would she do that?" What he's saying makes no sense.

"She didn't like me very much. I'd go as far as saying that she hated me, well after what happened between us. I always got the feeling that she wanted me out of Harper's life." He gives a light shrug. "Either way, what I did with her was stupid, and I blame myself for everything that happened after. I should have known how deeply hurt Harper was."

"It's not your fault, Brett. Harper pulled that trigger, not you. You didn't know what she was capable of. And I'm just glad that I'm alive." I feel a knot forming in my stomach at the mention of Harper. I still can't believe she would go to such lengths to frame me and try to kill me. "How are the twins doing?" I ask. "Who are they staying with?"

"They're staying with Harper's grandparents for now. I spoke to them a few minutes ago, and they just sounded confused."

"Yeah. I'm sure it's all hard for them to understand everything that happened." It hurts me so much that I can't be there for them right now, to comfort them. I place a hand on his shoulder. "What now, Brett?"

"Like I said, I called you here because I want to make things right." He points to the envelope on the nightstand. "In there is everything you need to know about your baby. I'm so sorry but he really *did* die. Inside there is his death certificate and a coroner's report."

When I was told that my son had died, I was shown a death certificate, but at the time I didn't want to believe it. Now, however, holding the envelope in my hands, I can feel the weight of reality settling in. It all feels like a final confirmation. When Brett told me the truth when I confronted him, I believed him then too. I know my baby is gone.

"Can you tell me what really happened?" I struggle to keep my voice steady. What I'm asking is probably all in the envelope, but I want to hear it from Brett himself.

He takes a deep breath. "It was the middle of the night when he was admitted to the hospital with a high fever. It was quickly managed, but the day before he was supposed to be released, he was found unresponsive in his hospital cot. Doctors tried everything they could to save him, but it was too late. They suspected SIDS, sudden infant death syndrome." Everything he tells me now is nothing new. I've heard it all before, but I thought they were lying to me. Brett's voice wavers as he continues. "I wish there was more I could have done. I should have been there for you."

I clutch the envelope tightly to my chest, trying to hold back the sobs that are threatening to escape me. "I guess I also have to stop running from the truth. Maybe it's time for me to finally get the closure I need."

Brett uses all the strength he has to reach for my hand and squeezes it. "Maybe I can help with that."

EPILOGUE

TWO MONTHS LATER

My baby is buried under the shade of an oak tree, his grave marked by a simple rock painted in the color of blood, on the farm I grew up on. The place I never thought I'd return to. I kneel down to get a closer look, brushing my fingers over the rough surface of the rock.

Memories flood my mind. The pain of losing my child, the fear I felt whenever the man I was forced to marry was near, and the desperation to escape. I remember the hopelessness that consumed me when I thought I had lost everything. But now, seeing this rock, I feel at peace, knowing that my baby is at rest in a place that will never be forgotten.

A river flows gently nearby, soothing my troubled heart, offering solace from the pain and the memories. I look up and see the great oak tree stretching its branches wide, reaching for the sky. It seems to be a symbol of life, standing strong and tall despite everything that has happened on this land, the tears that have watered its roots.

I sit down on the grass, my back against the rough bark. For the first time since leaving this place, I feel a weird sense of belonging. It's strange how much the place has changed and how much it hasn't. It's a relief not to see any children with pregnant bellies or old men prowling around, looking for their next child bride. Instead, I spot a woman getting out of a black BMW and making her way to me.

"You must be Christa," she says when she reaches me, and shakes my hand. "I was told that you were coming. My name is Sandy. I'm sorry I couldn't be here earlier to welcome you. I had a little car trouble."

Sandy is in her mid-to-late forties with a friendly face, bright hazel eyes, and a warm smile. Her short black hair is neatly combed back from her face and her suit is tailored to her frame. She stands tall and confident, her grip strong as she shakes my hand. She smells like a mix of lavender and citrus, with a hint of something musky underneath.

"That's okay. Thank you for agreeing to let me look around. I hope you don't mind that I already started exploring a bit," I say, gesturing toward the oak tree.

"Not at all." Her expression grows serious. "I heard that you grew up here. It must be hard for you to come back." Sandy coughs. "I'm sorry for what you went through. I did hear about what happened on this farm, and you must think I'm crazy for buying the land from Brett Lawson. But I'm a believer in new beginnings and I want to be one of the first people to create new memories in this town. I'm actually turning the farm into a rehabilitation center for women who have been through similar experiences."

I stare at Sandy in disbelief. I had thought this farm and the others in this town would be abandoned after everything that had happened there, but to hear that it's being used for such an important cause is enough to tug at my heartstrings.

"That's amazing," I manage to say, my voice quivering. "Thank you for doing something like that."

She pats me on the arm. "You're welcome."

Sandy's words about the rehabilitation center for women like me give me hope.

Despite all the tragedies that have unfolded under the oak's watchful gaze, suddenly I know what I'm going to do.

"Sandy, can I help in any way? I'd love to contribute."

Her face lights up with surprise and she clasps her hands together. "Are you sure? That would be marvelous!"

"Yes, absolutely." I'm determined to assist Sandy in her mission. I want to be a part of something positive, to help other women who have suffered and felt the same pain as I did. That way I can also be close to my baby's resting place, and honor his memory by making a difference in the world.

I will not stay in Bluefort, but I will build a life for me and Heather in Goldwater, the nearby town where Emily grew up.

Even though we barely know each other, Sandy pulls me into a hug. "You will be an invaluable addition to the team."

Before I leave, I return to the oak tree by the river one more time, unable to pull myself away just yet. "I need just a few more minutes," I tell Sandy.

"Take all the time you need. There's no rush at all."

The moment I sit down, my phone rings inside my handbag. I don't answer right away, but the phone continues to ring until I do.

"Christa? It's Angela, James's sister. I wanted to let you know that he was found dead in his cell three days ago. I found your number in one of the letters you sent him."

"Oh my God." My stomach bottoms out as the news sinks into my mind. "James... He's dead? How... what happened?"

"He had a heart attack," Angela tells me with a sorrowful voice. "The guards tried to revive him, but he didn't make it. Among his things, there was one letter written to you. If you give me your address, I can mail it to you."

"No," I say quickly. I can't wait that long to hear what his last words to me were. "Do you think you could read it to me over the phone?"

Angela hesitates, clearly taken aback by my request. "Sure, if that's what you want." I take a deep breath as she begins to read the letter.

Dear Christa,

I'm sorry for not returning your letters. The truth is, I could never find the right words to say to you. I've rewritten this letter at least a dozen times and it never feels right.

Telling you that our daughter, Heather, is beautiful didn't feel like enough. But I guess I have to settle for that one simple word. It hurts that I will never have the opportunity to be a father to her, and I'll forever be grateful to you for giving her what I cannot. But I have a favor to ask of you. Please don't ever tell her who I really am and what I did. When she's old enough to understand, perhaps you could tell her that you and I were a fling you had while on vacation in Austria and you do not even know my name. Tell her anything you want but the truth.

I never want her to know that her father is a murderer. I want her to grow up pure and innocent, without the burden of carrying my sins with her.

As for you, lovely Christa, you deserve a better life, and I hope you find happiness and love with someone who can give you that. Please take care of yourself and our daughter, Heather. I will never forget you and what we almost became.

By the time Angela finishes reading the letter, I'm sobbing uncontrollably. After the call, I think of my daughter. We've been through a lot, she and I, but I know that someday, somehow, we will be okay.

The same goes for Brett, who's now focused on his daughters while his wife is facing the consequences of her actions, and

Wyatt, who I visit at least once a month in a juvenile detention center in Cove Haven, Vermont.

Different people. Different lives. Different struggles. But we all have one thing in common. We are survivors, and we will do whatever it takes to keep moving forward.

A LETTER FROM L.G. DAVIS

Dear readers,

I want to say a huge thank you for choosing to read *The Nanny's Child.*

It was a joy to be able to continue Christa's story, and to help her find closure and some semblance of peace in her chaotic life. Putting a character through so much hardship and then giving them some sort of resolution is always a rewarding experience, and I hope you enjoyed reading the continuation of her story.

In my next books, I look forward to bringing you more compelling characters and plots that will keep you on the edge of your seat. To keep up to date with all my latest releases, just sign up at the following link. Your email address will never be shared and you can unsubscribe at any time.

www.bookouture.com/l-g-davis

I hope you loved *The Nanny's Child* and, if you did, I would be very grateful if you could write a review. I'd love to hear what you think, and it makes such a difference helping new readers to discover one of my books for the first time.

I love hearing from my readers. You can find me on my Facebook page, follow me on Instagram or Twitter, or visit my website. Please do contact me with any questions, feedback, or just to say hello. I look forward to hearing from you.

Thanks, Liz

KEEP IN TOUCH WITH L.G. DAVIS

http://www.author-lgdavis.com

ACKNOWLEDGMENTS

Writing a book, though rewarding, is a daunting task, and I'm so grateful for all the encouragement, feedback, and guidance I received throughout the process.

My heartfelt gratitude goes to my family, specifically my husband and children, for being my pillars of strength during the challenging process of writing and editing this book. Throughout the years, your unwavering support inspired me to grow as a writer.

I'm also grateful to my editor, Jennifer Hunt, who pushed me to create the best version of this story possible. Her insightful feedback and guidance were invaluable in shaping this book into its final form.

To the rest of the Bookouture team, thank you for your dedication and hard work in bringing this book to life. From the cover design to the marketing strategy, every detail was handled with care and expertise.

Last but not least, I want to thank my readers for giving me the opportunity to share my passion with you. Without you, this book wouldn't be possible. You are the reason why I write, and your support motivates me to keep telling stories.

I want to give a special mention to Carina Powers, who had my back during the writing of this book. Carina, thank you for taking on whatever tasks I was unable to do as I focused on writing Christa's story and could not think of anything else. Your support and understanding made this entire process easier for me. This book is dedicated to you.

Everyone else who has supported me on this journey, whether through kind words, beta reading, or simply believing in me, thank you from the bottom of my heart.

Made in the USA
Middletown, DE
22 September 2023